From The Women's Press Ltd
34 Great Sutton Street, London EC1V 0DX

Becky Birtha's first collection of short stories was *For Nights Like This One: Stories of Loving Women* (Frog in the Well, 1983). Her stories and poetry have appeared in a number of literary and feminist journals. She currently lives in Philadelphia, where she is working on a novel.

Becky Birtha

Lovers' Choice

The Women's Press

First published in Great Britain by
The Women's Press Limited 1988
A member of the Namara Group
34 Great Sutton Street, London EC1V 0DX

First published in the United States by
Seal Press, P.O. Box 13, Seattle, Washington 98111

British Library Cataloguing in Publication Data is available

ISBN 0 7043 4117 4

Reproduced, printed and bound in Great Britain by
Hazell Watson & Viney Limited
Member of BPCC plc
Aylesbury Bucks

Some of these stories were previously published in the following publications: "Johnnieruth" in *The Iowa Review*, Volume 12, Nos. 2/3 (Spring/Summer 1981), and in *Extended Outlooks: The Iowa Review Collection of Contemporary Women Writers* (Macmillan, 1982).
"Baby Town" and "The Saints and Sinners Run" in *Hear the Silence: Stories by Women of Myth, Magic and Renewal*, edited by Irene Zahava (Crossing Press, 1986).
"pencil sketches for a story: The Gray Whelk Shell" in *Common Lives, Lesbian Lives*, No. 6 (Winter, 1982).
"Her Ex-Lover" in *The Things That Divide Us*, edited by Faith Conlon, Rachel da Silva and Barbara Wilson (Seal Press, 1985).

We gratefully acknowledge permission to quote previously published material:
The lines from "The Lake Isle of Innisfree" from *The Collected Poems of W. B. Yeats* (Macmillan, 1982) are reprinted with permission of A. P. Watt Ltd. on behalf of Michael B. Yeats and Macmillan London Ltd.
The lines from *Where the Wild Things Are* by Maurice Sendak (The Bodley Head, 1967) are reprinted with the publisher's permission.

Contents

Acknowledgements

The work on this collection was made possible in part by an Individual Fellowship in Literature which the author received from the Pennsylvania Council on the Arts in 1985.

The author would also like to express her appreciation for the assistance of the students and faculty of the Master of Fine Arts in Writing Program at Vermont College, and of the members of her feminist writers support group.

Johnnieruth

Summertime. Nighttime. Talk about steam heat. This whole city get like the bathroom when somebody in there taking a shower with the door shut. Nights like that, can't nobody sleep. Everybody be outside, sitting on they steps or else dragging half they furniture out on the sidewalk—kitchen chairs, card tables—even bringing TVs outside.

Womenfolks, mostly. All the grown women around my way look just the same. They all big—stout. They got big bosoms and big hips and fat legs, and they always wearing runover house-shoes, and them shapeless, flowered numbers with the buttons down the front. Cept on Sunday. Sunday morning they all turn into glamour girls, in them big hats and long gloves, with they skinny high heels and they skinny selves in them tight girdles—wouldn't nobody ever know what they look like the rest of the time.

When I was a little kid I didn't wanna grow up, cause I never wanted to look like them ladies. I heard Miz Jenkins down the street one time say she don't mind being fat cause that way her husband don't get so jealous. She say it's more than one way to keep a man. Me, I don't have me no intentions of keeping no man. I never understood why they was in so much demand anyway, when it seem like all a woman can depend on em for is making sure she keep on having babies.

We got enough children in my neighborhood. In the summertime, even the little kids allowed to stay up till eleven or twelve o'clock at night—playing in the street and hollering and carrying on—don't never seem to get tired. Don't nobody care, long as they don't fight.

Me—I don't hang around no front steps no more. Hot nights

like that, I get out my ten speed and I be gone.

That's what I like to do more than anything else in the whole world. Feel that wind in my face keeping me cool as a air conditioner, shooting along like a snowball. My bike light as a kite. I can really get up some speed.

All the guys around my way got ten speed bikes. Some of the girls got em too, but they don't ride em at night. They pedal around during the day, but at nighttime they just hang around out front, watching babies and running they mouth. I didn't get my Peugeot to be no conversation piece.

My mama don't like me to ride at night. I tried to point out to her that she ain't never said nothing to my brothers, and Vincent a year younger than me. (And Langston two years older, in case "old" is the problem.) She say, "That's different, Johnnieruth. You're a girl." Now I wanna know how is anybody gonna know that. I'm skinny as a knifeblade turned sideways, and all I ever wear is blue jeans and a Wrangler jacket. But if I bring that up, she liable to get started in on how come I can't be more of a young lady, and fourteen is old enough to start taking more pride in my appearance, and she gonna be ashamed to admit I'm her daughter.

I just tell her that my bike be moving so fast can't nobody hardly see me, and couldn't catch me if they did. Mama complain to her friends how I'm wild and she can't do nothing with me. She know I'm gonna do what I want no matter what she say. But she know I ain't getting in no trouble, neither.

Like some of the boys I know stole they bikes, but I didn't do nothing like that. I'd been saving my money ever since I can remember, every time I could get a nickel or a dime outta anybody.

When I was a little kid, it was hard to get money. Seem like the only time they ever give you any was on Sunday morning, and then you had to put it in the offering. I used to hate to do that. In fact, I used to hate everything about Sunday morning. I had to wear all them ruffly dresses—that shiny slippery stuff in the wintertime that got to make a noise every time you move your ass a inch on them hard old benches. And that scratchy starchy stuff in the summertime with all them scratchy crinolines. Had to carry a pocketbook and wear them shiny shoes. And the church we went to was all the way over on Summit Avenue, so the whole damn neighborhood could get a good look. At least all the other kids'd be dressed the same way. The boys think they slick cause they get to wear pants, but they still got to wear a white shirt and a tie; and them dumb hats they wear can't hide them baldheaded haircuts, cause they got to take the hats off in church.

There was one Sunday when I musta been around eight. I remember it was before my sister Corletta was born, cause right around then was when I put my foot down about that whole sanctimonious routine. Anyway, I was dragging my feet along Twenty-fifth Street in back of Mama and Vincent and them, when I spied this lady. I only seen her that one time, but I still remember just how she look. She don't look like nobody I ever seen before. I *know* she don't live around here. She real skinny. But she ain't no real young woman, neither. She could be old as my mama. She ain't nobody's mama—I'm sure. And she ain't wearing Sunday clothes. She got on blue jeans and a man's blue working shirt, with the tail hanging out. She got patches on her blue jeans, and she still got her chin stuck out like she some kinda African royalty. She ain't carrying no shiny pocketbook. It don't look like she care if she got any money or not, or who know it, if she don't. She ain't wearing no house-shoes, or stockings or high heels neither.

Mama always speak to everybody, but when she pass by this lady she make like she ain't even seen her. But I get me a real good look, and the lady stare right back at me. She got a funny look on her face, almost like she think she know me from some place. After she pass on by, I had to turn around to get another look, even though Mama say that ain't polite. And you know what? She was turning around, too, looking back at me. And she give me a great big smile.

I didn't know too much in them days, but that's when I first got to thinking about how it's got to be different ways to be, from the way people be around my way. It's got to be places where it don't matter to nobody if you all dressed up on Sunday morning or you ain't. That's how come I started saving money. So, when I got enough, I could go away to some place like that.

Afterwhile I begun to see there wasn't no point in waiting around for handouts, and I started thinking of ways to earn my own money. I used to be running errands all the time—mailing letters for old Grandma Whittaker and picking up cigarettes and newspapers up the corner for everybody. After I got bigger, I started washing cars in the summer, and shoveling people sidewalk in the wintertime. Now I got me a newspaper route. Ain't never been no girl around here with no paper route, but I guess everybody got it figured out by now that I ain't gonna be like nobody else.

The reason I got me my Peugeot was so I could start to explore. I figured I better start looking around right now, so when I'm grown, I'll know exactly where I wanna go. So I ride around every chance I get.

Last summer, I used to ride with the boys a lot. Sometimes eight or ten of us'd just go cruising around the streets together. All of a sudden my mama decide she don't want me to do that no more. She say I'm too old to be spending so much time with boys. (That's what they tell you half the time, and the other half the time they worried cause you ain't interested in spending more time with boys. Don't make much sense.) She want me to have some girl friends, but I never seem to fit in with none of the things the girls doing. I used to think I fit in more with the boys.

But I seen how Mama might be right, for once. I didn't like the way the boys was starting to talk about girls sometimes. Talking about what some girl be like from the neck on down, and talking all up underneath somebody clothes and all. Even though I wasn't really friends with none of the girls, I still didn't like it. So now I mostly just ride around by myself. And Mama don't like that neither—you just can't please her.

This boy that live around the corner on North Street, Kenny Henderson, started asking me one time if I don't ever be lonely, cause he always see me by myself. He say don't I ever think I'd like to have me somebody special to go places with and stuff. Like I'd pick him if I did! Made me wanna laugh in his face. I do be lonely, a lotta times, but I don't tell nobody. And I ain't met nobody yet that I'd really rather be with than be by myself. But I will someday. When I find that special place where everybody different, I'm gonna find somebody there I can be friends with. And it ain't gonna be no dumb boy.

I found me one place already, that I like to go to a whole lot. It ain't even really that far away—by bike—but it's on the other side of the Avenue. So I don't tell Mama and them I go there, cause they like to think I'm right around the neighborhood someplace. But this neighborhood too dull for me. All the houses look just the same—no porches, no yards, no trees—not even no parks around here. Every block look so much like every other block it hurt your eyes to look at, afterwhile. So I ride across Summit Avenue and go down that big steep hill there, and then make a sharp right at the bottom and cross the bridge over the train tracks. Then I head on out the boulevard—that's the nicest part, with all them big trees making a tunnel over the top, and lightning bugs shining in the bushes. At the end of the boulevard you get to this place call the Plaza.

It's something like a little park—the sidewalks is all bricks and they got flowers planted all over the place. The same kind my mama grow in that painted-up tire she got out front masquerading like a garden decoration—only seem like they smell sweeter here. It's a big high fountain right in the middle, and all the streetlights is the real old-fashion kind. That Plaza is about the prettiest place I ever been.

Sometimes something going on there. Like a orchestra playing music or some man or lady singing. One time they had a show with some girls doing some kinda foreign dances. They look like they were around my age. They all had on these fancy costumes, with different color ribbons all down they back. I wouldn't wear nothing like that, but it looked real pretty when they was dancing.

I got me a special bench in one corner where I like to sit, cause I can see just about everything, but wouldn't nobody know I was there. I like to sit still and think, and I like to watch people. A lotta people be coming there at night—to look at the shows and stuff, or just to hang out and cool off. All different kinda people.

This one night when I was sitting over in that corner where I always be at, there was this lady standing right near my bench. She mostly had her back turned to me and she didn't know I was there, but I could see her real good. She had on this shiny purple shirt and about a million silver bracelets. I kinda liked the way she look. Sorta exotic, like she maybe come from California or one of the islands. I mean she had class—standing there posing with her arms folded. She walk away a little bit. Then turn around and walk back again. Like she waiting for somebody.

Then I spotted this dude coming over. I spied him all the way cross the Plaza. Looking real fine. Got on a three piece suit. One of them little caps sitting on a angle. Look like leather. He coming straight over to this lady I'm watching and then she seen him too and she start to smile, but she don't move till he get right up next to her. And then I'm gonna look away, cause I can't stand to watch nobody hugging and kissing on each other, but all of a sudden I see it ain't no dude at all. It's another lady.

Now I can't stop looking. They smiling at each other like they ain't seen one another in ten years. Then the one in the purple shirt look around real quick—but she don't look just behind her—and sorta pull the other one right back into the corner where I'm sitting at, and then they put they arms around each other and kiss—for a whole long time. Now I really know I oughtta turn away, but I can't. And I know they gonna see me when they finally open they eyes. And they do.

They both kinda gasp and back up, like I'm the monster that just rose up outta the deep. And then I guess they can see I'm only a girl, and they look at one another—and start to laugh! Then they just turn around and start to walk away like it wasn't nothing at all. But right before they gone, they both look around again, and see I still ain't got my eye muscles and my jaw muscles working right again yet. And the one lady wink at me. And the other one say, "Catch you later."

I can't stop staring at they backs, all the way across the Plaza. And then, all of a sudden, I feel like I got to be doing something, got to be moving.

I wheel on outta the Plaza and I'm just concentrating on getting up my speed. Cause I can't figure out what to think. Them two women kissing and then, when they get caught, just laughing about it. And here I'm laughing too, for no reason at all. I'm sailing down the boulevard laughing like a lunatic, and then I'm singing at the top of my lungs. And climbing that big old hill up to Summit Avenue is just as easy as being on a escalator.

Baby Town

Mimi sat very still on the high back seat of the old Hudson. When her Aunt Berenice started up the car, it made a sound like it was trying to say its own name, but couldn't pronounce the "s." "Hudn, hudnnn, *hud*nnnnn," as the motor finally got going. Now it was Aunt Berenice's car, but before that it was Grand-daddy's. It was funny that his car was still alive, when he had been dead for a long time now. She wondered if Granddaddy, up in heaven or wherever he was, knew that she and her mother and sister were here in Virginia, visiting with Grandma and Aunt Berenice. She wondered if he knew that they were going for a ride in his car this afternoon, and if he minded. Did he know they were on their way out to his cemetery?

Anyway, he must like it that Aunt Berenice took such good care of his car, keeping the outside polished, and the inside always swept and brushed perfectly clean.

Against the back of her legs, Mimi could feel the soft rub of the gray-brown plush. The seats in Granddaddy's car were so deep that if she sat all the way back it made her legs stick straight out before her, as if she were a much younger child. She could see the toes of her Sunday shoes, their patent leather greased with vaseline, so that they gleamed even in the dull interior of the car. They were the perfect shoes, simple and unadorned, with plain round toes and a single strap—perfect little girl shoes, like the kind Alice in Wonderland, or any other little girl in a book might have worn.

This morning, all morning, she had felt, magically, as if she really were a little girl in a book. They didn't let her wear her hair out, yet, but this morning her grandmother had combed it into soft, twisted plaits that were much thicker than the way her mother made them. She had looked in the big oval hall mirror afterward and felt a touch of excitement. Usually looking in a mirror was a kind of disappointing surprise. She never looked the way she felt inside, like somebody special and not at all ordinary. But this morning, the part slanted off to one side, the hair lay flat and shining pulled back from her face, and the big, puffy braids hung almost to her shoulders. She looked like someone else. Like somebody that something magical and special might happen to at any time, maybe even this afternoon.

If she shifted a bit on the car seat, there was the comforting crumple of crinoline, her best slip, the one with the lace around the edges, and the double-tiered petticoats. And she loved the white dress, with its yards and yards of sheer fabric gathered into the skirt, and the delicate pink flowers embroidered along the edge of the yoke. It was much prettier, she thought, than Mindy's dress, which was longer and more grown-up looking, but not nearly so full.

She glanced at her sister, Mindy, who sat at the other end of the seat, separated from her by the old-fashioned arm rest that pulled down out of the seat back to make a big bulgy cushion between them. Mindy was watching out the window, lost in her own thoughts, her long legs doubled up beneath her with no particular regard for the wrinkles that that would make in her dress. Mimi faced forward again and leaned back, carefully, not to dislodge her hat.

In the front, the grown people were talking to each other, grown-up talk. "A whole lot's changed since you and Lewis left." Aunt Berenice was talking to Mommy. "This whole section—" she gestured out the open window, then returned her gloved hand to the wheel, "this whole section, Violet, from here to the city limits. And almost all of them have been sold."

"And it's the nicer class of people moving in, too," Grandma Devereaux put in.

Without even paying attention, Mimi knew who they were talking about—what they always talked about: colored people . . . and white people. She concentrated on the houses they were passing, with their triangle roofs and big square picture windows. In front of one, a lady who looked like Aunt Berenice was holding a very chubby little boy by the arm, and locking the front door.

"Nice *respectable* people," Grandma was emphasizing. "Family people."

"You remember Jim Parsons, from Hampton? He and Ella just bought a lovely little place. It looks just like a picture post-card. . . ."

From her place on the back seat, all Mimi could see were the backs of the three women's heads. But those were so different from each other she might as well have been looking at their faces. All three of them wore their Sunday hats. Aunt Berenice's had a huge wide brim, with bunches of little apples and bananas around the crown. She must have picked it out on purpose to look as dif-ferent from Grandma Devereaux as she possibly could. Grandma's hat was small-brimmed, plain, black, and looked very severe and proper, pinned firmly with two fierce pearl hatpins to the coiled gray braids that wound around her head. Mommy's small blue hat, fitted close to her head, the faded bunch of lilacs on its side, bobbed between the other two, dodging every now and then to keep clear of Aunt Berenice's flaring brim.

Mimi put her hands up to touch her own hat, a white straw one with two ribbons tailing down the back. It looked a little bit like the hats that the girls wore in *The Five Children*. Everything about her was perfect today, she decided. Except maybe her knees.

She examined them now. There were still scars on them that were years old. There was a rough, round one that came from the time Mindy pulled the wagon around the corner too fast, when Mimi was three. Was it ever going to go away? At least her legs were smooth and shiny, set off against the dust-colored seat. There wasn't a trace of ashiness left on them. But they were a very dark brown. Much darker than Mindy's—maybe darker than her mother's. She felt a slipping, sinking feeling. Maybe it wasn't any use, to be all dressed up. . . .

Still, Deacon Carter had said this morning after church that she was pretty. Well, he had been talking about Mindy, too, but that was all right. He had said to Aunt Berenice, "Miss Devereaux, who are these pretty little ladies we have visiting with us this morning?" As if he didn't know. He had made a show of taking his glasses off and putting them back on again. "So these are Mrs. Devereaux's granddaughters. Aren't they lovely?" And he had taken and shook her white-gloved hand, and then Mindy's, while his voice seemed to boom out over the whole church. "They're turning into real young ladies, aren't they? And how old are the young ladies now?"

Aunt Berenice had nodded to let her and Mindy know that even though it didn't sound like he was talking to them, they were supposed to answer. "I'm nine," Mimi said.

"And I'm eleven."

"Nine and eleven!" Deacon Carter drew it out, with his voice full of awe, as if nobody had ever managed to get to be such ages before. "Nine and eleven." And then, to Aunt Berenice, "It's a shame Mr. Devereaux couldn't be here with us this morning. I'm sure he would have been pleased."

Sometimes Deacon Carter came into Grandma's shop. He was likely to ask a whole host of Sunday school questions, while he waited for his clean shirts or his freshly pressed suit. Because she and her sister had Bible names, they always got asked about their namesakes. Did Mimi know who Miriam had been, in the Bible? What chapter was it in? Could she recite any of the verses? Mindy's first name was Martha, so Mindy always got asked all about who Martha was.

She remembered last summer, when Deacon Carter had come into the shop. Mimi had been all prepared and confident, the verses in her mind. Exodus Chapter Two, Verse Four. "And his sister stood afar off, to wit what would be done with him."

But this time Deacon Carter had folded his arms across his chest and said, "Well now, little lady, I want to know if you can answer me this. I want to know if you can tell me what the word 'integration' means."

He unfolded his arms and clasped his hands behind his back as he looked down on her. His gold watch chain and the gold that framed his glasses glinted and flashed at her. His tufted eyebrows looked like two question marks. How quiet it had suddenly become in the shop. The constant, choppy-choppy sound of the treadle of Grandma's sewing machine had ceased, in the corner. The big old press that her Aunt Berenice operated seemed to have stopped its hissing and spewing, seemed to be holding its breath. She could feel them all watching her, watching and waiting, like Deacon Carter. She had to think fast, trying to stretch what she knew into the kind of definition that teachers were usually happy with.

His big, deep voice spoke again. "In-te-gra-tion," he enunciated slowly, just like a teacher giving a spelling test. "You're big enough to know what that means."

"It means . . . it's when . . . when you take two different kind of . . . things . . . and . . . and you mix them all up together."

He stared at her, through the thick square glasses. Then he pronounced, "It's when you take little white children, and little colored children, and send them all to the same school together. *That's* what integration is."

She had flamed with embarrassment. He kept on looking at her as if to say, "Now. What do you think of that?"

He thought she didn't know, but she probably knew more about it than he did! He thought he was so brilliant, standing up there over her like he was the superintendent of schools himself. Well, *she* lived in Philadelphia, where colored and white were just words—that was all—just words to describe the color of somebody's skin.

Finally Aunt Berenice came bustling up with the brown paper cleaner's bag that held Deacon Carter's shirts hoisted on the end of her pole like a Sunday school banner. She laid it crackling across the counter, and Deacon Carter pulled out his wallet and forgot all about Mimi. She had been free to escape behind the counter, bruised and angry, yet still feeling horribly embarrassed, as if she had done something wrong.

That was a year ago, and she still felt embarrassed. Why couldn't she forget things like that? What did she have to go and remember it today for, today when all she wanted was to feel pretty, just like . . . *any* little girl.

Now the car was pulling in through the gates, under an elaborate arch that read, "Restland Park." The talk in the front seat had changed. "I never did believe it." Aunt Berenice was shaking her head, the big brim of her hat swiveling back and forth. "Papa wasn't *that* sick. If he'd been able to get the kind of care he needed, he'd still be alive today."

"Now just stop, Berenice." Grandma Devereaux sounded exactly like a mother—nobody else could talk to Aunt Berenice that way.

Mimi remembered that she *was* Aunt Berenice's mother, as well as Mommy's mother. "Those white doctors don't know a bit more than our Doctor Peterson. . . ."

There it was again. No matter what they started out talking about, they always ended up on the same thing. She was never going to be like that when she grew up.

"I know, Mama, I didn't say that. It's the quality of the hospital I'm talking about. All that old, antiquated equipment. Junk so obsolete Riverside Hospital didn't have any use for it anymore—but the county figures it's good enough for us. And the facilities! You saw the room they had him in, with those uncovered pipes going right up the wall over his bed, dripping all the time. . . ."

Mimi could scarcely remember her grandfather's death. There had been hurried packing, and the long drive at night. Then the familiar house, crowded with strange uncles and aunts she had never met, but who all somehow knew who *she* was. The aunts all seemed to be fat, and to be wearing dark shiny dresses. They'd crushed her against their stiff, slippery fronts and asked, "You don't remember me, do you?" Everything had been all mixed up, with Aunt Berenice sleeping downstairs on the sofa, and the lady from next door cooking in Grandma's kitchen. She and Mindy had not been allowed to attend the funeral.

Now Aunt Berenice parked the Hudson, and the five of them started slowly along the winding gravel road in the hot sun. The grass on either side of the road was parched brown. All over it were scattered the rectangular blocks of stone, some sharp-edged and shining, others so worn they could scarcely be read. Mimi walked side by side with her sister, a little ahead of the grown ups. She tried to imagine, or remember, what her grandfather's stone was like.

"See that big marble pillar, Violet, with the angel balancing on one foot?" Aunt Berenice's strong voice carried clearly across the short distance between them. "That's what Geraldine Lacey put up for her mother."

"Geraldine Lacey chose that?" Mommy's voice was surprised. "I never would have expected her to pick out anything so. . . ."

"Garish?" Aunt Berenice suggested.

"Well, yes, I guess. And she was always so . . . thrifty, too."

"Thrifty!" Grandma Devereaux rolled the "Thr" and made the "ty" a sharp little tack. "Thrifty! Downright stingy is what I'd call it. If that girl really wanted to do right by her mother, she might have started sooner. It would have meant a good deal more to Myrtle Lacey if Geraldine'd spent some of that money on her when she was alive. How could a body rest in peace, anyway, with all that marble hanging there right over your head?"

Mimi caught Mindy's eye, and they both walked a little faster to get far enough away so that no one would notice the giggles. It seemed like you ought to be serious in a cemetery. You ought to be feeling sad and thinking about the people that had died.

"Do you think," Mindy asked after a little while, "that the dead people can see us, and they're all watching us?"

Mimi couldn't help looking around. But there was no one in sight—just the three grown ups, far behind them now, and farther behind, other cars pulling in at the gate.

"I mean, what do you think *happens* to you after you die? Do you think you can still *know* things?"

"I don't know." She tried to think about how it might be. "Maybe it's nice. Maybe you can fly, and be invisible, and it's kind of like magic." When she was a very little girl, after Granddaddy Devereaux had died, Grandma had told her that now he was an angel up in heaven and he was watching over her. But she wasn't sure if even Grandma believed that. She couldn't picture Granddaddy doing anything as undignified as flapping a pair of wings. And she'd never seen him in his nightgown—he always had at least a bathrobe on. But still, she wasn't sure that he *couldn't* see her, in a different sort of way.

"Maybe they *can* see us. Maybe they're around us all the time, just kind of watching everything, like a play." It must be hard to do that, and never be able to join in, never be able to say anything. There must be things that they wished they could tell you. "Maybe," she said suddenly, intrigued with the new idea, "maybe when you're thinking about somebody that's dead, it's really *them* thinking about *you.*"

"But what if there's nothing," Mindy said, a devilish spark in her eyes. "What if you stop breathing and that's it. The End. Finished. Point Blank. Nothing."

She didn't believe it. It couldn't be like that. It was too scary to think about, and in her head she quickly chanted over the words to the Bible verse, ". . . that whosoever believeth in Him should not perish. . . ." She wanted to talk about something else.

She said quickly, "How many different names can you think of for cemetery?"

"Graveyard," Mindy said promptly.

"Park."

"Park! That doesn't count."

"It does, too. The sign when we came in said Restland Park."

"O.K.," Mindy conceded. "Um . . . burying ground."

She had to think hard, and then she remembered. "Churchyard."

"That's only when it's beside a church."

"Well, a lot of times they are."

"This one isn't."

She looked around her, searching for more ideas. Now they were passing something that looked like a little house, built into the side of a slight hill. With a peaked roof and snug double doors, it looked almost cozy. A railing surrounded it, and a bit of hedge.

"Mindy!" She nudged her sister's arm. "Remember when we used to think cemeteries were Baby Towns?"

"Hey, yeah. I'd forgotten all about that. We *did* use to call them that. I wonder why."

"Don't you remember? We'd always be passing by in the car, and it looked like they were little cities and the gravestones were little houses. And we thought only babies must live there, and that was why everything was so small. I remember I used to think that was why they always had a fence around them, too, so the babies would be safe."

She could still picture the babies living here, quite free and happy, all by themselves without anybody to tell them what to do. She could picture them running about in diapers or little white nightgowns, perching on the headstones, or curling up to sleep in the shade under a rose bush, with their thumbs in their mouths. And at night, little flocks of them would disappear into those snug little houses. It would be like Never-Never Land, and she could visit, like Wendy Darling.

The babies would run away laughing if anyone tried to catch one. But Mimi would be able to. It wouldn't be easy. She would sit for hours outside the little house where it lived. She'd keep very still and sing soft lullabyes. It would hear them from where it hid and, after a while, it wouldn't be frightened any more. She'd bring it toys and surprises, and leave them for it, right there under that crepe myrtle. Sunday after Sunday, she would come back, until it knew that she loved it, and it would let her take it home.

"Mindy! Mimi! Girls! Right over here." The grownups had stopped, and crossed the brittle brown grass to one of the plots.

The gravestone was not remarkable. It was simple, plain but dignified, a little on the large side. Sure enough, her grandfather's whole name was carved neatly into the smooth flecked granite: Samuel Curtis Devereaux. The whole thing seemed so solid and permanent, so frank and matter-of-fact in the sunny daylight, it made her feel safe. Here was where her grandfather was buried. Here was his gravestone with his name on it. Here it would always be.

She tried to remember Granddaddy Devereaux. When he was

alive, he had always made her feel safe, too. She had watched him at the shop, clamping the big press shut with his long arms, while it steamed and hissed, pumping its big flat pedal with his foot. He was the one who lifted the clothes down from the wires with the long wooden pole, and did all the things that Aunt Berenice did now.

In the house, at night, when she'd still been afraid of the shadowy stairway, and the gaping dark hall that waited between the top of the stairs and the bathroom, she could remember Granddaddy Devereaux going up the stairs with her, hand in hand. And when they'd got to the top, he'd lifted her up so that she could pull the string on the light herself. She wished she could re-member more.

In the bathroom, over the sink, Granddaddy's shaving mug and brush and razor sat on the glass shelf, right where he'd left them. She knew his things, now, better than she had known her grand-father. Once she had sat in his chair upstairs in Grandma's bedroom, when nobody was about, and tried to imagine what it felt like to be him. There was a hollow indentation in the smooth leather of the seat. And the chair itself had the odd, somber smell of old leather and dust, old rooms shut up and seldom used, old books — that always seemed to Mimi to be her grandfather's smell. But that had been only last summer, and long after he died. . . .

"I wish he could have seen the girls now," Aunt Berenice said. "He would have been so proud of them."

Would he? Mimi wondered. Proud of what? Would he have been proud of them for looking pretty? Somehow, she didn't think so. For having grown up so much? But everybody grew. It was something you couldn't help, and so couldn't really take any credit for. Maybe he would have been proud that they had gone to church this morning. . . .

"Can me and Mimi — May Mimi and I go and explore for a little while?" Mindy turned from Mommy to Aunt Berenice to Grandma. You were never sure, when you were here, which was the right one to ask.

"Explore!" Grandma blew it out in a sharp little puff.

But Aunt Berenice said, "You mean just walk around for a little bit, by yourselves? I don't see any reason why not."

Now everybody turned to Mommy, and Mimi watched her glance from Aunt Berenice to Grandma before she came back to Mindy. "You know to keep on the paths, don't you? And keep your voices down. . . ."

Mindy was already off, her long legs striding in big loping steps. Mimi had to skip a little, to catch up. She caught a whiff of that excitement returning, what she had felt this morning looking in the hall mirror, and again in the car, that feeling that something different and special might still happen to her today. And that she was ready for it, special enough to meet it. The skirt of the white dress flounced around her with each skip, and the hat ribbons bounced and tickled the back of her neck.

On the other side of the gravel road, across a little ditch, was a section where the grass seemed even sparser, even drier than everywhere else. It was mostly just patches of dirty sand. The headstones were much smaller and there was no sign of the elaborate birds and crosses. The shrubbery and flowers that had set off some of the other plots were missing here, too. What was even stranger was that the plots seemed to be shrinking in size. Some were scarcely a yard long.

Mindy stepped right in front of the headstone of one of these shrunken plots, and read the inscription out loud. "Sandra Ann Waters. 1953 to 1957. Nineteen fifty-seven!" She repeated with surprise. "That was only last year!"

Mimi subtracted in her head. 1953 from 1957 left. . . . How could that be? Four years? "She was only a little girl." But how *could* that be?

And Mindy said exactly what Mimi was thinking. "How do you suppose she died?" They looked at each other, the wonder of it drawing them in close.

Mimi turned back to the lettering in the stone. Sandra Ann. "They must have called her Sandy."

"Maybe she had pneumonia," Mindy said. "I know. Maybe she had leukemia."

It was so strange to think of a dead person being a little girl.

There must be plenty of people who had known her, who were still alive. All her playmates. And maybe she'd had a sister. Would her sister have been allowed to go to the funeral? Did she get to have all of Sandy's toys and dolls, afterward? If anything ever happened to Mindy, Mimi would take good care of her dolls. And her Sunday dresses, when she grew into them. What had Sandy's parents done with *her* dresses? "I wonder what she looked like," she said aloud.

"Well, she must have been colored, because Grandma said this is a Negro cemetery."

"So what?" Mimi had flared. What did Mindy have to say that for? She sounded just like a grownup.

Mimi plunged past her and on to the next plot, loudly reading the inscription on its stone. "Linda Christine Washington. Suffer little children to come unto me: for such is the kingdom of heaven." She went on to another. "Otis Mobley. 1945." And now she came to a plot where there was a freshly heaped mound of earth—but such a *little* mound! She stopped suddenly, the understanding finally coming to her. They were all children—that was what was wrong. This next one, right before her. . . . She stepped closer to read it, and then backed away. "Baby Girl Johnson," it said. "1958." Baby girl—she had not even lived enough of a life to be given a name!

They were spread out all over both sides of the path, more and more of the little plots. All those children—more than all the kids on her block back home—all those children—dead.

She spun around and took another narrow path, one that seemed to be headed back. She walked quickly; she didn't want to read any more. But the words seemed to flash out at her as she hurried by. "Beloved daughter of Charles and Mary Danby." "Beloved Son." "William Nathaniel Bishop. 1949 to 1951." In spite of herself, she stopped. Nineteen forty-nine. Her stomach plunged. Nineteen forty-nine was the year she had been born.

She glanced around, hoping she would find Mindy beside her again. But Mindy was crouching over another stone several yards away, her back to Mimi and the hem of her white dress hanging in the dust. Away across the road, Mommy and Grandma and Aunt

Berenice were still standing there back where she had left them. Grandma had put up that black umbrella she always carried for a sunshade. Aunt Berenice was fanning herself with her hat. The three of them looked small against the great, bright sky. Nobody was looking her way.

Without her being able to help it, her eyes slipped back to the carving on the stone. Nineteen forty-nine. It could have been her.

She whirled about and fled back down the path. But it wasn't leading the way she'd come from. All of the paths, now, seemed to veer off at crazy angles and run wherever they pleased. And the graves weren't laid out in neat orderly rows anymore but seemed to go every which way—end to end or crosswise— jammed together in no pattern at all. She had to pay close attention not to step in the wrong place by mistake.

She felt surrounded—as if all that crowd of children were there, silently watching her. And then, abruptly, the path drew up short and ended.

The last two small graves were side by side against a rusty wire fence. Above one was erected a simple wooden cross—two sticks of wood nailed together and sunk in the sandy ground. Above the other was a thick plank, also wood, cut with a rounded top to imitate a headstone. Both of these markers had been painted white, and on both the paint was worn away, so that only faint traces still clung to the dull ashy brown of the wood. The two little graves lay side by side, as if the babies they sheltered might have been kin—they might have been sisters. If they had had names, no one would ever know what they were.

She couldn't stop staring at the bare wooden cross, at the plank that already leaned lopsidedly forward. It wasn't fair! It wasn't fair that this was all there could be for these two babies. All there would ever be for the rest of eternity. Old worn out sticks of wood stuck off in a corner by a rusty wire fence. No rose bushes or surprises or lullabyes, no snug little houses in a town all their own, nothing else pretty ever again. And it wasn't just because they were poor, either—she knew it wasn't only that. There was something else. The real reason was that they were colored. And this was what poor colored babies got. In the end, it *did* matter, after all. Everybody got sorted out, and here was what you got. This was how they treated you.

She stood over the improvised markers for a long time. She wanted to run away, but she couldn't move. Her hands clutched at the black plastic strap of the Sunday pocketbook. Inside the white gloves, her fingers were moist and sticky, the fabric damp between them. The sun beat down on the crown of her hat, and the thick braids hung like fur on the back of her neck. She could feel the droplets of sweat running at her temples and standing out on her upper lip, feel the sweat sticking her underclothes to her body, under the too-tight bodice of the stiff white dress.

She pulled way over into the corner on her side of the seat on the ride back, and shut her eyes. She could still feel the tears all plugged up in a salty lump that strained against her throat, feel them stinging the backs of her eyelids.

She wouldn't let anybody make her go for a Sunday drive, ever again. If they tried to tell her she would have a good time, it would be a lie. If they said they were going to a nice, pretty place, that would be a lie, too. Next time, they would just have to let her stay home.

She didn't want to see anything out the window, and she didn't want to hear anything anybody said. But Grandma Devereaux was talking. "Go around the block, Berenice," she said. "Go past the new school. I want Violet to see where the girls would be going to school, in case she should ever decide to come back here to live."

"Are we maybe going to come back and *live* here?" Mindy asked.

Mimi opened her eyes. Mommy was shaking her head, saying quickly, "Oh, no."

"That school's going to be integrated, you know," Grandma said to Mommy.

Why couldn't they stop all that talk? Why couldn't they ever just hush?

"And the school board's just as provoked as they can be. They thought they were getting off the hook by building us a new school." Aunt Berenice chuckled. "You can bet if they had known they would have to integrate, they would have saved themselves the trouble."

Mimi had a sudden urge to throw back her head, open her mouth wide and yell and yell and yell. Make all the noise she could and cover up everything they said. Fill in every little crack with noise, so that the whole car would be just a solid block of loudness, blaring down the road. She would be loud and bad and rude and just let her voice stream out on and on so that nobody could say anything else, ever again.

She shut her eyes again, squeezing them tight. She bent her head down, and put her thumbs up under the fat braids and held her ears shut. The voices, the car motor were gone. But there was still another sound left, thrumming loud in her stopped-up ears. It was the sound of her own blood, roaring like the ocean.

Downstairs, they were setting the table for dinner. She could smell the yeasty rolls browning, and the smell of the ham hock cooking in with the fresh greens. The aroma wafted up to her through the grating in the floor that Grandma had told her was there for the heat to rise through and warm the upstairs in the wintertime. If you looked down through the grating, and were quiet about it, you could see everything that was going on in the dining room, without anybody knowing you were watching them. But Mimi did not get up to look now.

She could hear, anyway, what was going on. She could hear the silver, the heavy pieces of flatware that had been in the family since the Spanish-American War, clanking together as the drawer under the table was pulled out. And then the clink of the thick, ornate china plates being taken from the glass-doored cupboard. She could hear Mindy laying them, one by one, with a muted thud, on the cloth covered table. She could hear all their voices, Mindy's voice rising above everything.

"Isn't there a law about it, that says people have to be buried in a cemetery when they die?"

Somebody answered in a low voice, Mommy or Aunt Berenice.

"But doesn't it cost money to buy a . . . don't you have to pay to get somebody in?"

A surprised laugh. More low answers, explanations, corrections.

And then, "Well, what happens if somebody dies and the person's family doesn't have any money—but the person is already dead?"

She couldn't hear the answers. She was glad she couldn't hear. She already knew what they were, anyway. In her mind, there was still the stark image of those two little graves, side by side under the bald wood of their makeshift markers, out there beside the rusty wire fence. She would never, never forget it. It was almost as if some part of her would always be out there too, unsheltered and exposed on the flat sandy ground, out under the open sky with them.

Downstairs, the grownups and Mindy were still talking. She didn't listen. She drew her knees up and wrapped her arms around them, leaning far back in the Granddaddy chair. In another minute they would be calling her. She would have to go. But for a little bit longer she was safe and hidden, here between the angular arms of the old chair. She curled up even closer.

The familiar scent rose all around her—the scent of old leather and dust and something like . . . shoe polish . . . waxy and warm. It was such a long ago smell. . . . It was almost like having someone with her, holding her. Someone who had seen what she had seen, and who understood. She leaned her face against the back of the chair, pressing her cheek to the soft, worn, ancient leather that was smooth and brown and comforting, like skin.

Ice Castle

I

Gail. Gail Fairchild Jenner. The same Jenner as the city coun-cilman for the West Side. The same Fairchild that the library up on the campus was named for. White Anglo-Saxon Protestants. The Bourgeoisie. What the hell was she doing in love with some-body with a name like that?

Only Maurie didn't know those things at first. She met Gail up on the campus, at the Women's Center, and thought she was just anybody. Somebody going to school part-time at night, somebody halfway poor—just anybody.

Maurie was not a student any more. She'd been out of college a year now. Before that, working the whole time, it had taken her seven years from start to finish. She figured Gail's life might be something like her own.

Gail wore big round glasses. Her large hands kept pushing the short, light brown curls back away from her high forehead, and the curls kept falling back to cover it anyway. Gail was tall and long-limbed, in the standard blue jeans everyone wore but Maurie—who was always coming from work—and an Aran knit sweater Maurie should have known was expensive, only she was thinking Gail would have made it herself. So there was nothing, really, to give Gail Fairchild Jenner away.

"My name's Gail—Gay." Could she really be that obvious—or that naive? Gay—was she? Was that the point? Now she was laughing, and Maurie was confused. I won't call her that. I'll call her Gail.

And what else had Gail said? Maurie strained to recall every word. It was at the Women's Center's annual poetry reading, and Maurie had been the last to read.

She loved giving readings—that was the one time when she felt completely visible. For all her colorfulness, for all her beads and bangles and bright batik prints, most of the time she felt that other people didn't see all of her. They saw only what mattered most to them at the time—her race, or her gender, or perhaps her age—and then didn't bother to look any further. It was only when she was on stage, standing up among a room full of attentive listeners, that she felt all her colors leap into focus.

Here in this wintry city, surrounded by pale, restrained faces, her full-blown features and deep colors felt like a rich, tropical ripeness. Her tan skin, freshly oiled, held the faint smell of coconut and glowed beneath the sliding silver bracelets that rang against one another when she lifted her hands. She could feel the same glow in her face. The trade beads and cowrie shells that she had braided into her hair swung and clattered softly against one another. And the soft lamplight picked up all the colors in the woven fabric she wore around her shoulders—the saffron yellow, the green, the earth red and the black. At times like this she felt thoroughly visible and utterly sure of herself, high and happy and perfectly loveable.

She loved reading last because she felt like the spotlight stayed on her, a lingering aura, long after the program was over. Her words would be the ones that echoed in people's memories; she would be the one they came up to talk to over the wine and cheese. And maybe some night some new person would come, excited by her work, curious about her life. . . .

She balanced her Wheat Thins and mozzarella cheese in a napkin and turned around to find Gail standing before her, long-legged and spare in the loose, bone-colored sweater, a spill of tousled brown curls capping her face.

"You're good," was the first thing Gail said.

"Thanks," Maurie said, smiling, pleased. And Gail was smiling back, her gray-blue eyes keeping Maurie's with an intensity that held her connected, in spite of the chattering crowd. So that Maurie waited, knowing they had more to say to each other.

"Why do you write poetry?"

It was a question nobody had ever asked after a reading, and it took her so unexpectedly that Maurie told the truth without thinking. "Because I want people to love me."

Gail let out a gasp of surprised laughter. "Seriously? Does it work? Do they?"

"I don't know. . . ." Maurie was suddenly self-conscious. "They don't tell. . . ."

"No one has ever walked up to you after a reading and said, 'Hey.'" And for a moment everything stopped and hung, precarious. "'I've fallen in love with you.'"

Maurie stared, caught in the storm-colored eyes. Gail stood so close that Maurie could inhale the faint, warm scent of her skin, damp beneath the layers of jersey and wool. She was still smiling, but now the line of her smile was a question, waiting.

How did we start talking about this? Who *is* this woman, and why is she asking me this?

"I didn't mean I'd expect somebody to do that." She was losing ground, the performer's sureness and self-confidence ebbing away. She turned back to the refreshment table, and Gail was right beside her, filling Maurie's Dixie cup from the half-gallon jug of wine, and then filling her own.

"But you'd like it if someone did." Her voice was too low, too familiar, and Maurie backed up a step. What was going on? Was Gail coming on to her? Was this how women . . . got started? She was confused, nonplussed, yet at the same time still pleased.

"Well, everybody wants to be loved." But what she was thinking was that all the poems she had read that night had been about women. She had planned it that way as a matter of course, because this was the Women's Center. But all those women in the poems. So what must this Gail think? Maurie took a swallow, the purple liquor sharp in her throat.

"And you . . . fall in love with people very easily."

No one ever talked to her this way. Gail's words, the closeness of her seemed to demand an answer. Her expectant eyes were like a wide, wet winter sky. "Yes," Maurie admitted. "Yes, I fall in love with people all the time."

"Maurie, hi. I really like that one poem you read—about the old woman in the bandana, on the bus, and how she used to be the prettiest girl at all the dances. . . ." She was aware of the event again, the festivity. That whole business with Gail had scarcely taken a minute. No one had even left yet. But now Roberta was asking her, "Do you want a ride? I have to leave now, because I promised Gary I'd pick him up after his class."

"I don't think I'm ready to leave yet. But thanks, anyway." She said it with no idea how she would get back to the West Side. Of course, she could take the bus, but they ran so seldom after nine at night. She pictured the dark, deserted corner where she'd have to get off the Main Street bus and wait for the Twenty-six. There was nothing there—just the tall iron fence and wide gates of the cemetery behind her, and the flick of car lights cruising across her body, one after another. She knew it wasn't safe. She didn't care.

There was the rest of the social thing spinning out. She talked to the other readers, to women she remembered from her English classes. She drank Chianti in the Dixie cup and listened, asked questions and answered questions, and watched Gail across the room, drinking Chianti, too, but standing alone. It was plain Gail was watching her, was waiting, too, for this to be over.

The crowd gradually thinned, quieted, until the last women had their coats on, at the door, and one of them looked from Gail to Maurie and said, "You two got a way to get home?" *You two.* At the same time they both said yes, and the woman who'd asked them said, "O.K. I need to drop these evaluations off at American Studies, and then I'll be back to lock up. But if your ride comes before that, could you just make sure the door's shut tight?"

"*Do* we have a ride home?" Maurie asked, after the others were gone.

Gail nodded, added, "We might have to wait awhile. My sister's supposed to pick me up." Gail dropped down on the couch at the side of the room and stretched out. Maurie hesitated, then sat down crosslegged on the floor near the end of the couch. She leaned against the wall. The room that had been crowded too small a few minutes before was suddenly vast and silent. She couldn't take her eyes off Gail's curly head, lying on her sweater-clad arms. . . .

"Maurie." It was the first time Gail said her name. "Maurie, do you ever fall in love with women?"

"Oh, yeah. At least as often as I've fallen in love with men." That muddled everything. Why had she brought up men? She wasn't being clear. But it wasn't clear, anymore, even to her. She *had* fallen in love with men. And women, too. She would try to tell what was true. "I've fallen in love with women lots of times. But nothing's ever come of it. We never did anything about it. Or maybe they didn't feel the same way. . . ."

She'd often imagined it otherwise—the woman with whom things would go differently. A woman her age, or maybe a little older, with the same experiences behind her. Who'd already been through college, and communes, and consciousness-raising groups, and was through with all the double dealing and disappointments that went down with men. Who was just as ready, now, as she.

"Maurie, how old are you?"

"Twenty-five."

Gail sat up on the couch and drew her kees in suddenly to her chest. "How old do you think I am?"

"I don't know." She began to look at Gail closely, at the smooth unblemished complexion, the gangly, still awkward limbs.

"Younger than me," she said slowly. "Maybe twenty-one or . . . twenty."

"I just turned seventeen last week."

The sister who came didn't look anything like Gail. The dark fringe of bangs that edged straight across her brow gave her face a scowl. Or maybe that scowl was because of Maurie. . . . In the dark car, in their bulky winter clothing, the three of them sat squeezed together in the front seat while the radio played AM inanity. She could tell when Gail turned toward her, feel her eyes on her. It was too dangerous to turn and meet them; she kept her focus out through the windshield.

There had been no snowfall to speak of yet, this year. The dry, scant flickers that were falling now would not stay on the ground. Still, Gail's sister steered the big station wagon carefully through the deserted streets. In Gail's family, there were still another sister and three brother Jenners. Six altogether. They'd be all over the West Side!

Maurie tried to think of the things to say that the sister might expect from her. But she felt slow, flushed and heavy-headed, too stoned. She wished desperately that she and Gail could be alone. Gail's mittened hand lay against Maurie's corduroy covered thigh—loosely, casually, staying.

II

As much as Maurie hated the winter, hated going out in the cold, three times in three days she walked up toward Chapin Parkway. Her face burned in the assault of the wind; her toes froze after the first five minutes. She walked toward the block of the Parkway where Gail lived—only five blocks from Maurie's apartment—coming closer each time, and then going home. The third time she walked past the house. It was stone, set back in a deep lawn, with a drive curving around the side. It seemed to have hundreds of windows, all of them polished bright and shining like magnifying glasses.

She felt outrageously conspicuous. In her life, among people she didn't know, she often felt exotic. She liked that feeling, to be someone special who stood out from the crowd. But in this neighborhood, even though there was not another person on the block, she felt garish and outlandish. The color of her skin felt like a sunlamp burn—over-exposed and wrong. The beads she had braided into her hair seemed artless, and the colors in her skirt, the bright lacings in her knee-high boots, loud and gaudy. She kept her eyes focused straight ahead, and did not look to see who might be watching from those many windows.

Gail had given her a phone number, but she couldn't call her. Not at home. Among all those people, the odds that Gail would pick up the phone were only one in nine. Who could she tell them she was?

Evenings when she stayed in her apartment, she sat by the window, waiting, watching the sky darkening into that deep, luminous blue—a long half hour. Then indigo. Then night. Outside in the alley, the wind whipped and wheeled, rattling the glass, shrieking and whistling round the corners of the building. She was glad there was still no snow. But without it the winter seemed even more relentless.

Nobody would be out walking on nights like this. She could come. She could bundle up so well that no one would recognize her anyway. And no one would see her turn down the alley, slip in at the downstairs door. Come on Gail. You have to come here. Because I can never come to you. A white woman, a younger woman could maybe get away with it. Show up some Saturday afternoon in Nikes and a baggy sweatshirt, just "Tell your Mama and your Papa I'm a little schoolgirl, too." But not Maurie.

Saturday night she turned the radio to the blues show that came on every week. She was drinking vin rose. She might as well keep on, and get drunk by herself. It seemed appropriate. It was late, going on eleven, when the phone rang.

"I couldn't call you before. My brother Ted listens to everyone's phone calls. This family is like the headquarters of the FBI. My kid sister Wendy snoops in my drawers all the time. And my mother's just as bad—always finding excuses to poke around in my room. Daddy just 'checks up'—you know, finds out from neighbors and friends of his where you've been seen and in the company of whom. I hate living in this family!"

"Sounds familiar." Maurie grinned into the receiver. "I couldn't wait to go away to school." She'd had to pay a high price for that privilege—waiting tables, typing, through the summers and the semesters, too.

"I wanted to live in the dorm, but they wouldn't let me. They think I'm too young. And anyway, they're not going to pay room and board for me to live at the other end of the same town. Not that they couldn't afford it."

"Listen," Maurie broke in. "Can we . . . did your brother go out tonight? The one who listens to your calls, I mean."

"Oh, I'm not at home."

"Where are you?" She pictured Gail standing in a telephone

booth while the traffic passed and the wind stormed at the glass walls. There was a pay phone on the corner of Elmwood Avenue, half a block away. Maybe Gail had forgotten exactly where Maurie lived. . . .

"I'm babysitting tonight. The kids finally went to sleep."

"Oh. Babysitting."

"You have a regular job, don't you?" Gail's voice was wistful. "What do you do?"

"I teach. At a co-op pre-school." For a second she thought about the children in her class, their parents. . . . What would they think if they knew what she was up to? What *was* she up to? Trying to seduce a seventeen-year-old kid?

"What about you?" she asked. "What are you doing in school?"

"Failing." Laughing. Nervous, embarrassed.

"Why?"

"I'm not doing it on purpose. I just—don't care about it enough. It's not that important to me."

"What is important to you?" Wishing she would say, "You."

"I don't know," Gail said. "I'm trying to figure that out. I'm real depressed a lot of the time. I drink too much. Sometimes I think I'm suicidal."

"Maybe you don't belong in school right now. Christ, you only just *turned* seventeen. You must be precocious as hell."

"But I'm *failing.*"

"That happens to a lot of people," Maurie said. "I failed courses my first year in college, too."

"But I'm supposed to be so spectacular. Everybody's holding their breath, waiting for me to distinguish myself. Since I refuse to be a social butterfly, I'm supposed to be a scholar."

"They *want* you to be a social butterfly?"

"You don't know my family," Gail said. "I mean, my mother sent me to etiquette school. And dancing lessons. Then, last year, I was supposed to be a debutante. We almost came to blows over that."

Maurie laughed. "You don't mean that, seriously?"

"Yeah, I do. Some etiquette, huh? She used to hit me all the time when I was little. Just over anything. Like if I left my stuff on the dining room table, or if I forgot to change my clothes when I came home from school. She was always hitting me. Now that I'm bigger than her, she doesn't dare. But she gets her way most of the time, anyway."

Her own anger flared up so fully and swiftly it surprised Maurie. She could see Gail as, maybe, a ten-year-old: an awkward, big-boned child who could never do anything right—blinking back tears from the red-faced sting of a full-handed slap. Those people. They had everything. Why did they have to hit a kid?

"My mother drinks even more than I do," Gail said. "I think she's an alcoholic."

"What about your father?" Maurie asked, finally.

"Dad's O.K., I guess. He's pretty liberal, compared to a lot of kids' parents. He doesn't try to run my life too much. He just doesn't understand—about this college thing—that this just isn't what I want to be doing."

"And what is it," she asked again, "you'd rather be doing?"

Gail was thinking. "I really love track," she said, after a little while. "I guess I'd just spend all my time doing sports if I could. Hey," her voice suddenly came alive. "Do you run?"

"No. . . ."

"Do you play tennis? Do you ski?"

Maurie sat holding the phone, wishing, for the first time in years, that she were somebody else.

After she hung up, Maurie thought over what more she knew of Gail now. Not much. Gail played the clarinet. Badly. But her mother didn't want her to quit. Gail had never held down a paying job in her life. Gail definitely did not belong in a ballroom. . . . But why hadn't Maurie asked the things she really wanted to know? Why hadn't she asked Gail if *she* ever fell in love with women? Or when she could see her again?

Gail called her once—twice again. From another sitting job, from the campus one night. No, her mother always expected her home for dinner. She'd want to know who the friend was, to meet her first. She was going on a skiing trip this weekend with her sister's youth group from church. She had exams to study for next week—final exams. It was a joke; she knew she would fail them all. But studying would look good, anyway. Her parents didn't have any idea—and the blow wouldn't fall until they got her grades in January.

"I didn't expect you to be home again on a Saturday night," she told Maurie. "Two weeks in a row. Don't you ever go out?"

"I guess I'm not much of a party-goer." But she had been asked to a party—over at Wendell's tonight. She'd forgotten, conveniently, wanting to stay home in case the phone rang.

"What were you doing?"

Drinking again. Wishing you'd call. Writing a poem about you. "Nothing."

The other nights—when Gail didn't call—would lag and creep. This was not the way she had expected this thing to go. She wasn't sure what exactly she had wanted, but knew this wasn't turning out to be it. Sometimes the tedium sent Maurie out of the house, hurled her into the early darkness to force her way against the wind, up Elmwood Avenue, toward the Parkway. The wind chill factor was often well below zero, but at least it hadn't snowed yet. The shops along the Avenue were open late, lit up for the holidays. Maybe Gail would have to do some Christmas shopping. . . .

Roberta and Gary lived on Elmwood Avenue. She hadn't called or stopped in to visit for a long time. She didn't do it now. What could she say when they asked what was going on in her life?

Wendell lived a few blocks down, on Lafayette. She could imagine his response. He'd pretend that he was trying to take her seriously. "Now wait a minute. Lemme make sure I get this straight. She rich. She white. And she *how* old? And you in *what* with this chick?" She had always thought Wendell was fun, had always laughed at the way he spared no one, nothing with his jokes. Now she felt like she had to protect herself.

Once, when she got off work at three-thirty, instead of going home she took the bus in the other direction—up to the campus. She wandered around randomly, then bought coffee in the

Rathskellar—where students who were failing usually hung out. Sitting alone, drinking her coffee, it occurred to her that the answer was to go away. She would go away for Christmas—back to Boston, to spend the holiday with her family. Maybe it would put this whole thing in a different perspective. Maybe she would forget all about Gail.

III

Then she came. Two days before Maurie was to leave for Boston, the phone rang—nine o'clock on Saturday morning—and she knew in an instant it was Gail. "Listen. I could come over this morning. My mother's out of town and Nancy and Ted are off in Williamsburg at my cousins'. I have to go to a music lesson this afternoon, but I have a couple of hours until then. . . ."

Gail seemed to take up all the space in Maurie's small, square living room. She sat on the couch—it was a day bed, really—and made the legs look spindly, rickety. She slouched down, and her long legs stretched most of the way across the floor. She had thrown the bright blue jacket on the only other chair, where it collapsed looking winded, with its arms flung out. Now Gail was rubbing the fog from her glasses in the folds of another expensive sweater—soft blue and green. In the daylight, her short curls looked more gold than brown.

"Are you hungry?" Maurie asked. "I mean, I was just going to fix myself some breakfast when you called. So I thought I'd wait to see if you wanted some too."

A wide smile. "What are you having?" An adolescent's insatiable appetite.

"Eggs and toast, and orange juice. I could make you eggs, however you like."

Gail was interested, had followed her into the narrow kitchen. "How are you having yours?"

"Poached."

"I'll have one, too."

She filled the saucepan and set it on the burner, began to slice the bread. "One poached egg on toast, coming up."

"No, just plain."

"Just plain? Just one egg? All by itself?" Maurie had never eaten a poached egg except on toast, in her whole life. "You don't want *any* toast?"

"Well, maybe one piece. On the side."

Her own eggs came out perfect, every morning. This morning she did everything the same way she always did, boiling the water and turning it down, then stirring to make a funnel in the center of the pot, slipping the egg from the saucer into the swirling center. But the white splayed out from the yolk and spread, in lumpy streamers, all through the water. She had forgotten to flip the timer, and as soon as she scooped the egg out, she knew it would be runny and underdone. It sat there, a pale and almost colorless blob, while the water ran off into a puddle around it, on the white china plate. She had forgotten the toast, and now it was scorched from her quirky, antiquated toaster, one side undone, the other crisp black. She forgot to put the salt on the table, too, didn't think of it until she sat down to eat her own egg—and Gail was already finished by then. There was no butter, because Maurie never bought anything but margarine. But Gail insisted that everything was fine.

Maurie had imagined this visit so many times. She had always thought it would be evening—the two of them surrounded by quiet jazz and soft lamplight. She had wanted Gail to be charmed by her tiny apartment, and the way she had decorated it—the brilliant African fabric that covered one wall in a sunburst of color, and the instruments: the big-bellied calabash with its shiny beads that hung from a strap on the wall above the chair, the tall conga drum in the corner. Sometimes when people came in they would start to play with the instruments. Almost no one could resist the kalimba, resist pressing a few notes from its flat metal prongs. And then, later, she'd thought that Gail might ask to see more of her poetry. . . .

But Gail was restless, moving quickly from the kitchen back to the other room, stretching her long legs out, drawing them in, taking off her glasses and cleaning them again, glancing from time to time out the window that faced on the empty alley. "Let's go out," she said.

"Out? But . . . it's freezing. It looks like it's going to snow."

Gail's eyes were excited, alive for the first time since she'd come. "Maybe it will!" And when Maurie joined her at the window, kneeling beside her on the couch, Gail said, "It was beautiful, walking over here. The clouds are so thick, and so low. . . . We can go over to the cemetery. There's never anybody there."

Never anybody there—to see what? Go to the cemetery—and do what? Go for a *walk*, in *Buffalo*, in *December?* Incredible as it seemed, she was pulling on her own sweater, her jacket, muffler, going out to walk in the cemetery, in the middle of winter, with Gail.

They walked side by side, following the wide road that led through the center of the grounds. Everything was frozen solid— the stiff colorless grass and the creek. It seemed as if their voices had frozen up inside them. There was no sound, except the crunch of the two pairs of boots in the gravel at the edge of the road, and now and then a bird calling.

They didn't touch. Yet Maurie could feel a kind of aura, like a magnetic field, surrounding Gail, as though there were electric in the blue of Gail's down jacket, a charged field that was tangibly alive, the closer Maurie's body shifted toward Gail's. She wondered if Gail could feel it, too.

Gail took long steps, her hands swinging at her sides, and stared straight ahead into the distance, at the bare lace of tree branches far off against the low gray sky. Maybe Maurie was wrong. Maybe Gail didn't feel anything. And nothing was going to happen—not today, not any other day. Maybe thinking that there was anything between them was just building castles in the air—fantastic creations spun from nothing—elaborate towers, tunnels and turrets, whimsical twists and turns. Elegant fragile architecture that simply wasn't there.

In the air—but what she pictured was a castle made of ice. High walls arched into vast doorways and cathedral roofs. Down long halls, footsteps rang like bells and echoed up the steep stairways, through the vaulted, empty rooms. Exquisitely beautiful— but not a place where anyone could live, not a place she could stay. The air inside—cold as crushed crystal, filling the lungs. The castle perfect, solid and sound, as shiny and smooth as glass. On the first day of summer it would be gone.

Gail's voice, disappointed, broke the silence. "It isn't going to snow. It's too cold." And then, a few steps further, "I have to head back. I've got to get to my lesson."

"Gail?" Maurie's own voice sounded as sharp, as penetrating as a bird's. A gulp of cold air slid down her throat. "Gail, are you a lesbian?"

There was a long, quiet stretch. They were going uphill, and she could hear herself breathing hard, the air coming forth in rhythmic puffs from her open lips. Finally Gail answered.

"I don't know. I've never been—involved with anyone. But I think it would be women—a woman—if I did."

Maurie didn't think before she said the next words—they just came. "Are you afraid of me?"

Gail turned to her, surprised. But there was something else— relief—in her face. "Yeah. You're right. Yeah, I guess I am."

"Of what? Why?" And when Gail didn't answer, just shook her head, she asked, "What do you think of me? I mean, who did you think I was? Why did you want to know me?"

Gail turned to her as if to explore Maurie's face for the answer. "I *did* want to know you. I mean I still do. But it was . . . you just seemed so different from me. I don't mean just . . ." she looked away, then back, "in the obvious ways. Well, maybe that's part of it, but it was more. There's a way you've got about you—standing up there reading those poems, you just seemed so sure of yourself, so absolutely you. All the while you were reading I kept thinking—I saw something in you that I wanted, wanted to have, wanted to be. . . ."

Gail's stride was still long, determined, the heels of her boots biting into the frozen gravel. But the pace had slowed. "When we gave you a ride home, and I saw where you lived, on that alley over that garage, all by yourself, I just thought you must have your life all together, exactly the way you want it to be. And then I couldn't imagine what you were doing trying to let me into it. I thought—I must have been wrong about you. I thought you'd know better than that."

"You think that little of yourself?"

More long, silent steps, slower. Gail's head was down now, eyes on the toes of her boots, and she didn't answer.

"So is that what you think of me, now? That I'm not all that wonderful after all, since I want to be . . . friends with you?"

"I don't know what to think any more." At the crest of the hill, as Gail raised her head, a draft of wind lifted the muffler at her neck, blew back the loose spray of curls around the edge of her face, and settled it back. They walked on. "I think, maybe," Gail said, "I'm not sure if I should see you again."

The words tumbled the world awry. Panic, fear flew flapping through Maurie like a wounded bird. "You don't want to see me again?"

"Oh, yeah. I'd like to. . . ."

The unspoken end of Gail's sentence hung in the air—the part that began with the word "but"—while the panic inside Maurie lurched and beat. She asked, "Because of your family?"

"No, not them." Gail flicked her head in a single, abrupt shake. "They can't run my life forever. I just don't want to—ruin it for you."

"Ruin how? Ruin what?"

"Anything—everything."

They kept walking, back the way they had come. Beside her, Gail's green woolen mittens swung at her sides, in the rhythm of her stride. Her face was downcast again.

The noise of traffic was audible once more—a long lean on a car horn, and now the loose, futile clanking of somebody's snow chains against the dry road surface. The Delaware Avenue gate loomed suddenly just a few yards away.

Maurie's face, her hands, even her toes were tingling with heat.

"Look," she said, the words crowding out in a rush. "You don't have to protect me. Maybe you don't like yourself all that much, but *I* like you. . . ." In Gail's face she caught her response—the quick flash of irrepressible pleasure. ". . .And I want to see you again."

At the corner of Gail's block they stood lingering awkwardly by the curb. As if she could hear the question in Maurie's mind, Gail said, "I'm going to be out of town for a couple weeks. I have to go to my grandparents' in Philadelphia, and then down to St. Croix. . . ."

"St. Croix!"

But Gail was shaking her head. "It's no big deal. We go practically every year. My whole family's going to be there—and believe me, they could ruin Paradise!"

"When will you be back?"

"Saturday before New Year's."

Someone came out of one of the houses on Gail's block, and they both grew suddenly alert, moved another foot apart—then caught each other's eyes in a sheepish smile. "I'm going away, too," Maurie said. "Down to Boston, to spend Christmas with my folks."

Gail laughed. "God, I wish I didn't have to do that. And you're going five hundred miles out of your way so that you can? Incredible!"

Now a car pulled into a drive at the far end of the street, and Gail half turned to go, squinting down the block.

"Will you call me when you get back, Gail?"

"O.K."

"Is that a promise?"

"I don't know. . . ."

IV

The child in the picture wore a crimson dress and carried a lunch pail in one hand and a schoolbag that looked enormous in the other. A complicated pattern of elaborate cornrows framed her penny brown face. Her wide smile was toothless in the front.

"Kasinda. The first day of school."

"That's right."

"This is priceless. Would you ask Aunt Laverne to get a copy made for me?"

"You can ask her yourself, Maurie. They'll be over tomorrow night."

"For dinner? The kids and everyone?"

"Kids and all. Laverne said I'd better not let you sneak out of here this time without her getting a chance to see you. She says the last time she had a good talk with you was that summer we were all down on the Cape at Joe Franklin's place. That was two years ago, if it was a day. Laverne wasn't even expecting Zaki yet." Maurie's mother moved back to the stove and lifted the lid on the pot roast. The aroma of onions and hot, meaty juices steamed out into the kitchen.

Maurie watched her movements, feeling half at home, and half like a guest. She always expected things in this house to look exactly as they had all the while she was growing up—when there was no money for new appliances and floors. But Pop and Uncle Jerome had redone the kitchen three years ago. And now, here was this modern, avocado-colored, six-burner range—and then on top of it that old blue and white mottled pot with the chipped lid, the one that had been on the stove Sundays and holidays ever since Maurie could remember.

Her mother, too, was a study in contrasts. The gray knit pants and yellow jersey would have looked as fresh and modern as the new kitchen, except for the faded print apron, ruffled and rick-racked, that completed her outfit. Maurie and Toby had given it to her for Mother's Day, some fifteen years ago.

"We ought to do that again. You could get down for a week or two in the summer, couldn't you?"

Yes, she could come back, year after year, and know exactly what to expect. But what if, one year, she didn't come? Or brought somebody with her?

"This ought to be done right on time. I just have to make up a pan of rolls and. . . ."

"I'll do the rolls." She uncovered the bowl of dough, searched under the sink for the square tin her mother always used. She tried to imagine Gail in this kitchen. Gail wouldn't know which pan to use for the bread, or the melted butter. Would her hands know how to shape rolls? Would she seem to take up all the space in this kitchen the way she had in Maurie's apartment? Would everything here look too gaudy and new, or too shabby and old?

When she cleared the table, she looked again through the pictures. Most of them were of the children—Kasinda and Kalil and their baby brother. There was one of her aunt and uncle together, in wet bathing suits, with their arms around one another. Something that simple. Just a picture of the two of you, at the beach last summer, to send home to the folks. . . . She squared the edges of the stack of photos and dropped them back into their bright yellow envelope. She wiped across the oilcloth with the damp dishrag.

At Christmas dinner the following afternoon, they were all there in person—along with her maternal grandmother, a great aunt and a second cousin. Her brother Toby had driven in from New Haven. Pop did almost all the talking, and still managed to eat most of the rolls. Mom ran in and out of the kitchen and never got around to taking off her apron. When the baby turned his bowl upside down and everyone laughed, Toby made a face at Maurie across the table and, down at the other end, Kasinda made practically the same face at Kalil. Everything going according to plan—everybody doing exactly what was expected.

And what would all the family do if she told them? Or somehow they found out? Looking around the table, she couldn't imagine a setting in which what she was contemplating could be more scandalous. Unless maybe it was *her* parents' house. What was Gail doing now? Were several generations of Jenners sitting down to a formal candlelit Christmas dinner in Philadelphia? Roast goose? Plum pudding? Champagne? Were they having a barbecue on a beach in St. Croix? Was Gail thinking about Maurie?

Finally, the next day, she got to sneak away with Toby. They drove into town and then over the bridge across the Charles, into Cambridge, parked the car and walked through the Common toward Harvard Square. Toby pulled his pipe from the wide pocket of his softly padded jacket. The bowl was already filled and ready to light. At home, he never smoked. She wasn't even sure if Mom and Pop knew he smoked a pipe. *She* had never told them.

He inhaled the first breath and blew it out in a blue puff. "God, it's good to get out of there. That place always makes me feel like I'm ten years old. It's like a time warp, every time I come back." She nodded and laughed along with him. "You'd hardly believe I was a fully functioning adult back in New Haven. Whatever Pop wants me to do, I end up going along with it. I can't say no to him any easier than I could when I was only four foot tall."

She remembered him like that—four foot tall—a skinny kid with a narrow chest who couldn't fight or even insult people properly, who got teased unmercifully for his sallow "yellow" complexion and his tight black curls, and who cried more easily than she did. Pop had always wanted Toby to learn to fight back. . . . She and Toby had never, either of them, fit in, but they managed to make it all right for each other.

In the summertime, when all the other kids were out playing, both of them carrying books home from the library together made it all right. When he started reading *The Daily Worker* every day, and going to the Du Bois Club meetings after school, she acted like that was perfectly normal behavior for a fifteen-year-old boy. When she wore her beads and peasant skirt and sandals, and a huddle of girls on a porch giggled as she and Toby walked by, and then one of them called out, "Hey girl! Don't you know they ain't no such thing as black hippies?" Toby pretended he hadn't heard a thing.

He had still been that skinny-chested kid, all through high school, but now—she watched him while he talked. Now his hands were big and competent looking, one of them waving the pipe around to accent his words. Now his chest was broad as a barrel, and his skin had weathered to a richer tone, like fine leather. Now there was a short thick beard, that matched the curls. She hadn't paid much attention to his changing, but today here he was—a grown man.

"Did you see me up on the ladder? Gee, I thought the whole

neighborhood was watching. I swear I thought I was gonna break my neck, perched up there with all those strings of lights draped around me. I felt like a blasted Christmas tree. You know where the steps are, at the front of the porch. Well, you can't set the ladder flat because of the steps. Pop's supposed to be holding the ladder steady; instead he's checking out all the extension cords going, 'Wait a minute—this ain't the right one here—no—this one don't fit together. . . .' I thought any second he's gonna plug in the wrong one, and I'm gonna light up and go blinking off and on. They can just leave me up here, and forget about Christmas decorations."

"Remember that time they were going out, and Pop was instructing us about what to do in case the Christmas tree caught on fire?" she asked, laughing.

"Yeah." Toby mimicked Pop's most serious face, and they both said it, chanting out in unison, just as they had in answer to Pop's question that night long ago. "Crawl under the Christmas tree and pull out the cord."

"I woulda done it too," Toby said, shaking his head. "I probably would do it today, if Pop told me to."

"What gets me," she said, "is how I feel like I can't talk about what's really going on in my life. Like they don't really want to know that I *have* a life, outside of them. So I feel like I'm only half real."

"Yeah, I know. Same here." He looked across at her, from under the Greek fisherman's cap that was pulled down low on one side, his familiar black eyes twinkling, set deep in the tan face. When they were kids, he used to claim he could read her mind. "So what really is going on in your life? You writing much?"

"Some." She hoped he wouldn't ask if she'd brought any of her new poems with her this trip. Lately, they were all love poems about Gail. She added, "Nothing terribly profound."

When she didn't elaborate, he went on. "How's your love life? You know—the big 'S'?"

She shook her head. "Nonexistent." But her face was suddenly hot. Nobody but Toby would have seen the subtle color change.

He looked at her closer, a smile widening his face. "You fell for somebody, huh? Or somebody fell for you."

"Cut it out, Toby. I'm entitled to a private life." Yet she really wanted to tell him. The way she'd been able to tell no one but him when she was twelve and that man in the car had stopped her to ask for directions, and she'd gone up to the window—how frightened she'd been when she saw he had his pants down all the way around his ankles. . . . She wanted to tell the way she'd been able to, years later, when she first had sex with a man, and Toby had reassured her that it was all right, that she didn't have to feel guilty, that passion was a perfectly healthy, moral thing to feel. The way he'd been able to tell her, when he was going out with a white girl—Rochelle Herman—when Maurie and Toby were both still in high school, and he trusted Maurie not to tell their parents, and she never did. And then, in New Haven, when he was living with Aileen. Maurie had gone and stayed with them, and thought of Aileen as a sister-in-law, those two years. But she never told.

"Who's the lucky guy?" he teased.

"It's nothing like that. It's . . . just a crush. A bad crush—that won't amount to anything." She could hear Stevie Wonder's voice singing accusingly. "You got it bad girl. . . ."

"You can tell," he said again. "We're all adults here."

I wish we were. Instead she said, "Isn't that strange, Toby? Isn't it? We *are* adults, finally—you and me. When I was a kid I used to look at Mom and Uncle Jerome sometimes, and think about how they were sister and brother, Toby, like you and me. And that now they were two grownups—but they were *still* sister and brother. And I couldn't get over that fact. It just used to amaze me. I always wondered what it would feel like, if it ever happened to us. And now here we are—a grown-up sister and brother. . . ."

"Crossing the Common in the chill December air," he struck a pose, pipe in hand, "trudging through the dry, decaying leaves, reminiscing about our lost youth. . . ."

"Yeah." She giggled. "Walking and talking—just a couple of boring grownups."

At the end of the day, after another company dinner, after a long evening of her father's stories, and his interminable advice, she sat on the bed in the little room at the back of the second floor. Yellow print curtains she had chosen when she was fourteen still hung at the window. The desk, unbelievably small and impractical, stood in the corner, and on the shelves above it were the few children's books that she had managed to get second hand, after falling in love with copies borrowed from the public library: Laura Ingalls Wilder, Edith Nesbitt, Marguerite Di Angeli. What a strange child she must have been growing up black in Boston, in the 1960s, and reading all the time of prairies and gardens and moors, about children from Sweden and England, writing poems about places she had never seen, and wishing she came from some exotic, faraway land, too—not being able to see who she was.

She remembered, she used to light the room with candles when her parents were not at home. The flickering flames made the colors dance in the psychedelic posters she had taped on the wall. That part had come later. But now it was all mixed up together with the little girl stuff. *Siddhartha* and *The Prophet* sat on the shelf right next to *A Little Princess*. A box of incense lay on the windowsill beside a cluster of china horses—God, her mother must come in here and dust this stuff every week.

She took a stick of incense from the package and lit a match to its end. In a curl of pungent sandalwood smoke, those last years came rushing back. How trapped she had felt in this room, burning incense and candles, how powerless to change anything about her life. It was easy, when she was here, to slide into feeling powerless again. Just like Toby had said. . . . But she hadn't really been powerless, even then. She had left home. . . .

She stood up and faced herself in the mirror that hung over the dresser. It was such a small mirror only her face showed. She hadn't wanted any mirror, in those days. It had taken her so long to learn to love herself, as she was.

But she did now. She studied the face framed in the square of dark wood, and she liked everything she saw—the thick eyebrows that she was glad she had never plucked, the wingspread nose and ripe, melon lips, and her coloring, sand tan like everyone else in the family. She didn't care anymore that her hair wasn't as "good" as Toby's. She had her mother's chin, long and proud. The neck of the robe opened to the beginning of the swelling of her full breasts. That was as far as the mirror would let her see. But she knew the rest, loved it all. Somebody else could love her too, if she'd let herself. . . .

She turned away from the mirror and back to the bookshelf, looking for something she could use to read herself to sleep. She pulled out a slim paperback volume of poems—Federico García Lorca. Later, when she had washed up and snuggled down under the covers to read, the book fell open of its own accord and a paper marker fell out. The place it had marked was the end of the introduction, written by an editor or translator, but quoting the poet's own words about himself: "I write poetry because I want people to love me."

It was the last night Maurie was there that it came up, completely casually, after dinner, while everyone was still at the table. Luckily, there were only the four of them that night, no guests.

"Guess who I saw in town this morning," Maurie's mother announced to the table at large. "Francine Albertson."

Maurie remembered the Albertsons—neighbors who had once been her parents' best friends, but had moved years ago. She remembered the children—Franny, with the stuffed panda bear she carried everywhere, and the ribbon always untied on her top plait, hanging down in front of her face. Jerry, in a too-big police cap, flinging out his arms to block the sidewalk, shouting, "Red light!" "What are Franny and Jerry doing now?" she asked.

Before her mother could answer, her father made a noise— somewhere between a harrumph and a sigh—shaking his head. "It's a shame about that boy. A real shame. He was such a good-looking kid, too."

"Jerry? What happened to him?" She imagined a car accident, or his face slashed up by a gang of muggers.

But now Pop had apparently said all he wanted to on the sub

ject. "Just fell in with the wrong crowd, I guess." That old adult/kid routine—covering up. And then just to their mother, exactly as if Maurie and Toby were a couple of pre-schoolers and simply wouldn't hear him, "I felt so bad for Al, when he told me. I didn't know what to say. I don't even know why he told me. What a thing to have happen to a man."

After he left the room, she turned to her mother, to find her suddenly busy clearing the plates from the table, her lips pressed together into a flat, tight line. She disappeared into the kitchen with her hands full, and almost immediately her voice rose in song.

> *"Jesus paid it all*
> *All to him I owe*
> *Sin had left a crimson stain. . . ."*

Maurie turned to Toby. "What was that all about?"

He met the question with that innocent smile of complicity they'd always shared. "He's gay," Toby said. "Jerry Albertson. I used to run into him on the campus sometimes, when I had that summer job at the bookstore." He glanced out toward the living room, where their father had turned on the T.V., then back at her. "I guess he came out to his old man."

She was stunned. She could not, for anything, think what would be the totally natural thing to say. Words stammered out. "Pop thinks it's that bad?"

"Yeah. All he can see is a blot on the old man's character. A failed father somewhere in the background. Fathers are responsible for everything, you know." He chuckled. Dropped his voice. "Mom has a much less Freudian outlook: It's a sin. Whatever the question was—Jesus is the answer."

She ought to be able to laugh along with him, joke about this. She hadn't see the Albertsons in ten years. None of them should matter to her, at all. There was a tremor in her voice, asking, "What do *you* think?"

"Me?" He shrugged. "I think it's the twentieth century. I've been to Greenwich Village."

She tried to steal a glance at him, and met his eyes. They were no longer laughing, but steady and thoughtful. She couldn't go on with this conversation, couldn't let him watch her face for another minute. He was too sharp, knew her too intimately. She got up and began to gather the serving dishes, following her mother into the kitchen.

So now she knew what it would be like. Mom would think she was a sinner. Dad would think he was a failure. Only Toby . . . but she could never tell, not even Toby. She'd have to lie to them for the rest of her life. It felt like lying already, like she'd been lying ever since she got here.

"You put the food away. I'll wash," she told her mother. And ran the water hard so she wouldn't have to talk just now.

V

Twelve long hours on the bus, to ask herself questions. Framingham, Worcester . . . not sleeping, watching the shopping malls and parking lots, and then the silent dark fields slip by. Springfield, Albany, Schenectady . . . unlit farmhouses, lighted cloverleafs, on and off the throughway . . . Amsterdam, Johnstown, Utica.

Of course, Mom had wanted her to stay. "I don't understand why you have to leave today, Maureen. It's only *Friday!* We've hardly even had a chance to see you. What do you have to go back so soon for?"

"I just need to be able to spend the weekend at home." She watched her mother's face draw in, at the word "home," and she hurried on. "I've got to have my lesson plans done by the time school starts Monday. The kids'll be really high, and I want to have my act together." Another lie.

Oneida. Syracuse. A couple of sleepy-eyed college students—a boy and a girl—gathered together their hats, backpacks, book bags, a stray glove, a guitar. Just the way they collected their belongings, either of them grabbing whatever was closest, made her think that probably they lived together. Stumbling groggily down the aisle, they looked too young to be sexually active, "living in sin," her mother would say. . . . A new thought pulled her fully awake. It was all right if both of you were kids. But if one was an adult, and the other—seventeen? There were laws, of course.

Did it matter? Being a lesbian was against the law, too.

She stared out through the glass at the sleeping streets. Somewhere along the way it had begun to snow. The windshield wipers slogged back and forth in a dull, blunt rhythm, and the questions licked and nudged at the edges of her mind. Was it taking advantage of Gail? Was it Gail, after all, that drew her? Or had she just needed a Gail, a someone . . . female . . .? What if nothing more happened between them? Would Maurie still end up a lesbian? Was she one already? Geneva, Canandaigua, all around the Finger Lakes, the long way home.

The woman next to her had fallen asleep and sagged over to take up three quarters of the seat. Maurie's knees and her back ached and there was a splintery knot in her neck. Rochester, finally. Only another hour now, along the canal.

Twelve hours in all, and no answers—only the long yearning to be home, the absolute certainty that the only place she wanted to be was in that gray city on Lake Erie that Gail would be coming home to, this same morning.

Letting herself into the apartment in the gray dawn light, she piled her bags in the kitchen just inside the door, slung her jacket over a chair. She'd meant to go right to sleep and sleep far into the afternoon, but her head was whizzing, whirring. She would put something mellow on the turntable, then brew a pot of camomile tea, and drink it while she read her mail, winding down.

After two cups, after opening all the Christmas cards, she was still on a zingy high. She felt as if she were still in motion, traveling toward some destination just a little beyond her. On her feet now, she moved from one end of the small space to the other, then back again, and finally to the window.

The sky was white, clearing. The snow was finished. Several inches deep, it clung in a curve to the window frame and hooded the fences and ash cans beyond. The alley was a canyon, filled with a river of snow, that would open to other snowlogged streets, flow past banks of bulgy white cars and bushes—everything soft and anonymous, the city taken by storm.

All of a sudden, she was flinging on her things again, pulling tight at her boot laces, drawing them criss-cross over one another, and then throwing open the suitcase, burrowing haphazardly through the Christmas gifts and toilet articles to find her warmest sweater. As she stepped outside, a gust of wind shoved against her back, and she lurched forward a few awkward staggers, then laughed and ran with it, letting it push her in a clumsy run through the drifts up the alley, and on to the Avenue.

Fifteen minutes later, her heart pounding, Maurie stood in the middle of the unploughed street and faced the stone house on Chapin Parkway. There was no one else on the block, no movement about the house. Huge icicles that sparkled like cut crystal hung from the rainpipes and eaves. In the pearl bright morning light, the many windows glistened like ice. There was no trace of the elegant curving drive that swept around the side, or the steps that led up to the main door, between the two tall columns. There was only snow—deep and unruffled, the yard one with the yard next door, the sidewalk and the street: an open sea of snow.

A moment ago, she had thought this her destination, where she was headed this morning once and for all. But her fingers and feet were tingling; she felt full and vibrantly alive, not yet at the end of this venture. She squinted a moment longer at the house, then took a deep breath. The air was as fresh as cold springwater. Her breath rushed out, and she couldn't stop the smile that took over her face. She turned from the house and pushed on, past it.

At Delaware Avenue, Maurie crossed the deserted street against the light, and slogged in through the wide-standing gate to the cemetery. Alone in the open space, she waded deep into the drifts, leaving her mark—trails and twists and figure eights, crazy spirals and mazes no one would ever understand. She sank knee deep in soft banks and slid on the frozen creek. At the top of the hill, where the wind had blown the road almost bare, she spun in dizzy laughing circles under the bright sky. She filled her lungs with the icy air, and called and shouted aloud, stuck her two fingers in her mouth and spurted out a whistle that frightened all the birds from a snow-laden evergreen. And then she sang—in a loud voice that cracked from the long night of silence—the first song that came to her, dancing in the snow.

With a stick broken from a fallen branch, she began to write, in huge letters through the fresh snow. First she wrote "I love you." It didn't matter if it didn't keep, if the wind or the sun erased it, or more snow fell to cover it up. Right now, this day, this hour, it was real, it was true—and wonderful. "I love you," she wrote again and again, leaving the message, a loud tell-tale secret, all over Forest Lawn. She drew hearts with arrows through them, crooked stars and crescent moons with sleepy smiling faces, wrote her name and wrote the words again.

It was fully daylight now; the sun had broken through. On a last clear patch of snow, by the fence on the expressway side, there was space for one more message. She drew a circle, and added the two more lines that turned it into a woman's symbol. And then another woman's symbol right beside it, overlapping, intertwined. She had seen that design displayed again and again at the women's center—on posters for upcoming events, in the newsletter, on buttons some of the women wore pinned to their clothing. . . . Now she understood that need to display it, to say it somehow.

Her toes were wet, even through her leather boots, her fingers and face numb. Bits of ice clung to her wet mittens, with the dank smell of damp wool. Heading back down the hill, she smiled at the message that greeted her everywhere. It suddenly struck her who the words were really meant for—how right it was that she should be the one to read them, over and over again.

She had made her own trail, and she followed it, the way she'd come—all the way to the Delaware Avenue gate. At the gate she turned back to gather in one last view of this new place, this play-land of sunshine and snow. But the city this Saturday morning seemed a new place too, shimmering and alight, friendly and full of promise, and still soft-edged and vulnerable under its coverlet of snow. A huge yawn pushed her jaws apart, and then another; a long sigh. She crossed the street and ploughed on toward Elmwood Avenue, toward the alley—coming home.

pencil sketches for a story:
The Gray Whelk Shell

The town is on an ocean and the bar is on the beach. The real reason I want to go back there—back to that town, that bar— is a woman. She's a character I want to capture, pin down. Bars, parties, Saturday nights—the few times I've caught a glimpse of her were in places like that. If I only went where I'd normally go— I'd never find her.

When I go looking for her at night, I'm Gabriel, the other character. It's really Gabriel who's interested in her.

How much do we know about her? I know only a little more than Gabriel. Gabriel knows:

— That she is deeply tan and sun blond, and the blond hair is short and very, very curly
— That she is full of bravado
— That she loves to dance
— That from the way she walks, anyone would know she was a dyke from a block away.

Beyond this, Gabriel knows the pale plaid shirt against the honey-colored skin, that precise tender edge where they meet, the collar open, throat exposed deep into a V, more open than Gabriel would ever wear one of her own shirts.

Gabriel does not even know the woman's name. She has invented a name for her—a silly, child's name that she says only to herself. But she has no one else to talk to about this preoccupation, anyway, and when she goes to the bar, she goes alone. If I tell you the name that Gabriel has secretly chosen for her, I'll have to say it very quietly: I'll whisper it: Curlytop.

I, at least, know another name for her. It is probably not her real name either, but it is what the others call her, the ones who greet her at the bar. They call her Piper, those women who dance with her.

Gabriel doesn't know how to dance. Nobody believes this, because Gabriel is black. No one, black or white, seems to believe that any black woman might really not know how to dance, might have to learn. Gabriel goes to the bar and she watches, trying to remain invisible. In this bar, in this town, in this year, it is easy for a black woman to stay invisible, not because she is unnoticeable, but because it is easier for the white women who come here to let her be. Almost all of the women *are* white who come here, to this town. Still, Gabriel stays here. She is centered like a small craft in this bay. She stays to take whatever the ocean yields her, stays for the beach and the mornings, for the sea and the sky.

These nights, in the bar, she watches, trying to memorize the motions of the others, trying to drink enough sweet pink wine so that it won't matter to her how her own body moves.

The bar is on the beach, its back room opening to a redwood deck that looks out over the water. The loud music swells against the sounding of the tide. Gabriel thinks that if she were down on the beach alone, or maybe with one other person, she might be able to dance to this music.

But when she walks out of the bar, she goes home. Goes home and puts on the radio to a station that she otherwise would never listen to, and tries to repeat what she's seen. Already it's hard to remember the steps, to relax her shoulders, to think what to do with her hands. . . . She does all right, really, until she catches sight of herself in the mirror—knows she could never do it in the bar. Gabriel turns off the radio and gets undressed and gets into bed. She brings herself to orgasm before she goes to sleep. Doesn't need to be drunk to be uninhibited enough to do that. She lets it happen slowly, rise to fullness, lets it flush her like a warm, salt tide. Savors it into sleep.

She returns to the bar other nights, many nights. Keeps watching. When she stands by the bar with her back to the dance floor, she drinks her wine very slowly and still watches—in the mirror.

Is this really Gabriel Rose, so hesitant: And so intent on doing things that she normally never does? I have asked her and she admits it: That it's hard, in this culture, to be a lesbian and to be alone. That if you want to meet someone, there are not so very many places to go. Where else *is* there, besides the bar? But she doesn't meet anyone at the bar, either. She is too shy there.

Then how do these two meet? Does it ever happen that their worlds cross? They cross every night that Gabriel sees her Curlytop at the bar. But Piper doesn't know that, does she? Has she noticed this dark woman watching her, memorizing her shoulders, her hips, her feet? Maybe.

Maybe yes. Maybe Piper asked her to dance one time. And Gabriel said no too shy and stumbled out of the place, face burning and maybe she didn't know (maybe) Piper followed her—followed her home.

The town is on an ocean, beached on an ocean bay. Drawn out in a long low stretch strung close against that shore. If you are like Gabriel, you remember the way the morning light can wake you, far earlier than in any other place. You remember the urgency to get outside, and the first smack of the wind, rich with salt, and running the path to the beach. The tide is low, the beach spread wide open, fresh-washed and nearly deserted. Far, far down the shoreline there's a tiny figure in a sea green dress, and far, far out over the ocean, there's a kite that's just a tiny speck of color in the huge blue sky.

That was Gabriel—the one with the kite. That's where she is at home—on the beach at sunup on a morning when the tide's almost all the way out. Flying a kite. Sometimes gathering seaweed. Or digging for shellfish. Immersed in her dreams.

This morning there's someone else on the beach, lying in the sand near that stretch where the shoreline curves in close behind the Anchor Cafe and the bar. Someone catching the sun awfully early, Gabriel thinks. No, not the way the person is sprawled face down on the sand. Derelicts are rare here. Anyway, the clothes—too clean. White pants. Some high school kid, some young punk who drank too much and passed out on the beach.

She keeps her distance, passes by, threading in and out of the water, following the tide line. She is looking for shells today, the bottom of her pail already covered with small jingle and periwinkle shells, fluted scallops and bright black mussels. She finds the most of moon snail shells. Half of them, when disturbed, reveal the furiously kicking legs of hermit crabs. She laughs and tosses those back to the sea.

Just as she is about to turn back, she sees something half submerged in the sand. Round, gray hump. Pear shape. Snub spire. A whelk shell. Crouching close, she fingers the ridged spiral, the smooth gloss of the opening. A knobbed whelk. It is whole and nearly perfect.

Walking back—the water is higher up the beach. She has to pass closer to the figure that is still sprawled in the sand. Sees it's a woman. Stops. Before the morning is out, the ocean will claim this place. Is she asleep? Is something wrong? Gabriel steps just close enough to be heard.

"Hey! The tide's coming in!"

The woman rouses, turns over, sits up. Rubs hands across eyes and pushes clumsy fingers through sandy hair, squinting up into Gabriel's face. It's Curlytop.

"What'd you say?"

"I said the tide's coming in." She tosses the words across the stretch of sand like a ring of keys. "I just thought you'd better know."

There seems to be no need to say more. She turns a quarter turn, moving the pail to her other hand and Piper says, "Wait a minute."

Gabriel waits.

"C'mere," says Piper.

She would love to. It's the way the woman says it that holds her back. She shifts the shells to her left hand again, and her eyes travel down the beach in the direction she was headed.

"I've seen you before—at the bar. Haven't I?"

The words draw Gabriel back to meet the recognition in the

woman's eyes, head-on. If she answers, her voice will give everything away. She nods her head.

"So, what about the tide? How high does it come?"

Gabriel points to the mark on the concrete breakwater.

Piper feels suddenly foolish, fragile. She can think of no suitable answer. Her eyes drop. Gabriel sees it, hears it in the voice that says, "Well, thanks."

Piper is out of her element; the snap, the authoritativeness are lost on this black woman who wears a dress and carries a bucket on the beach at some unthinkable hour of morning. It occurs to Piper that this is someone from a world she knows nothing about. Yet there has always been a crossing, a place where their two worlds intersected. Now there are two, morning and night.

If it were night now, Piper would know how to approach her. She would have had a few drinks, would be herself, with her own easy confidence. Not this newborn rawness like the sun too bright in her eyes. At night she could be assertive. It would be dark on the beach and no one would see them—she would move swift to surprise her. . . .

She forgets that there is no one to see them now. Forgets the nights when she'd had plenty to drink, when all she did was follow the woman home.

Gabriel is in charge now. She knows it, and she comes a step closer and sits in the sand in front of Piper because she wants to, folding her legs beneath the gathers of sea green cotton. She smiles. "How'd you get here, anyway?"

The way she says it makes Piper look down at herself, start to brush the sand off her favorite white slacks. They are hopelessly wrinkled, damp: so is the shirt, sticking to her. Gabriel is still smiling and she smiles, too, at herself. "I'm not even sure I know. Let's see, last night. . . ." She'd been with a friend. Carol had already made plans to go deep sea fishing this morning, and wanted to go home and get some sleep. Piper wanted to stay, always, stay until closing time. At that hour of the morning, it suddenly seemed too much to try to find her way through the town alone. . . . She doesn't tell Gabriel the real explanation—that what she can't bear is the having to go home alone.

"I knew it wouldn't be long until daylight. So I figured I'd sit on the beach a while and finish my beer—wait until I sobered up some. I just climbed over the railing onto the beach, and passed out just like that."

"I was afraid you were sick or hurt or something." Gabriel thinks: Isn't it funny? I would have stopped for any woman. I didn't know it was you.

"You thought I was already something the tide washed up, huh? Not just a pretty good candidate." This time Piper laughs aloud and a spike of pain drives deep into her head and keeps pounding there. She remembers how much she drank. It isn't going to work to be clever, witty, sparkling, with this hangover on a beach in broad daylight in wrinkled clothes she's slept in. She touches her palm against the throbbing in her temple. Gabriel is right next to her, squatting on one foot and one knee.

"What's wrong?"

"Nothing." Piper tries her smile again. It feels lopsided. Shakes her head—wrong move. "Just got a headache—a hangover."

"Would you like me to . . . try to get rid of it for you?"

Again Piper starts to laugh and stops. Not just because it hurts. She looks away. "Sure, if you want to try."

Gabriel sits behind her on the sand where Piper can't see her, can only feel the cool fingers touching her, searching out the place where the headache is lodged, gently pressing it out. She has to imagine how Gabriel looks, pictures her poised—knees bent with her feet out to one side, arms lifted, the ripe green falling in folds from her bare brown shoulders. What is the look on her face? Piper is afraid to imagine. There's only a faint skin scent like petals of roses, and she must interpret any message from the pliant, earth-colored fingers kneading out the night before, confident, competent. She would like to lay her head in this woman's lap and let those fingers send away all the nights before. Let the gentle hands go all over her until there has never been a time before this single sea-clean summer morning.

She has to ground herself, say something. Opens her eyes. "What've you got in the bucket?"

"Shells. You can look if you want."

The pail is half filled. They are delicate and tough, dull bright crumpled and smooth, many-sized shades of gray, brown, white. . . . Piper has seen shells before but she has never taken the time to see their differences. Fingers them, tracing the grain with her eyes half closed. Studies them like faces. Knows whose velvet sure touch has handled each of them. Somehow, this morning, she has fallen into the same hands. She could be a shell on the beach, picked up and taken home. . . .

"What do you do with them?"

"Make things."

"What kind of things?"

"Things that hang and turn and sound in the wind. And I put them in my macrame and weaving and make things to hang up in the windows."

"Did you make the one that's in the door at your house?"

Gabriel's fingers stop. "How do you know my house?"

"I wanted to find out."

Piper turns swiftly enough to catch the delight that leaps like a flame in Gabriel's eyes. Gabriel's face is only inches away. Her voice slides across thin ice. "What else do you know about me?"

Piper could have found out easily enough. The bartender, Ann, knew everyone, probably could have told her plenty. Perhaps she had just never admitted to herself that it was real that she was curious. "Not much. I don't know your name." She waits, sending the question deep into Gabriel's eyes that are clear and golden-brown, like a stream-bed when sun shines through the water.

Gabriel says, "Turn around and let me finish." Piper submits. She is still, listening for what the fingers may tell her. She can almost hear Gabriel smiling.

A gull cries out and cuts a high arch into the blue, soaring with wings scarcely moving. The sun is milder on her eyes now, pours across her body, pressing summer into her joints. When was the last time she was out at this time of morning? When she was a child?

She picks up another shell, conical, spiraling, soft gray. When she puts it to her ear the ocean answers, small and contained against the downbeat of the other ocean that is very close now. The shell is the only one of its kind. She holds it to her ear a long while. When she puts it down, Gabriel says, "That's a knobbed whelk." Then she says, "My name is Gabriel." She stops massaging, shifting her weight to lean on one arm in the sand, looking into Piper's face now, smiling still. "How's your head?"

Piper has forgotten that there is an explanation, a justification for this intimacy. Or there was.

Gabriel is putting the shells back into the pail. Then she stands and Piper stands too, has to balance herself as the headache threatens to surge in again. She feels anxious, seeking a way to stop this interval from ending. Keeps holding the gray shell. "Would you like to go get some breakfast or something—Gabriel?" Instantly she looks down at herself, the rumpled, disheveled state she's in.

Gabriel laughs. "That's all right. I've had some breakfast anyway." She takes a step toward the pail and Piper moves a step, too.

"Are you going home?"

Gabriel nods.

Reluctantly, Piper holds out the gray shell to be put with the others, but Gabriel doesn't take it yet. She says, "You can walk back with me if you like."

These two then, side by side. Piper's definitive, solid gait measuring Gabriel's—subtle, liquid, soundless. Even from far down the street they contrast. Piper is light and pastel, the disorderly curls sunbleached silver, her skin like winter sunlight beside Gabriel's vivid colors—deep bittersweet of the brown limbs against that succulent green flood, Gabriel's slate black hair cropped close and careful, the tiny, wiry curls melding to one softness. The two heads are close. I can't hear what they are saying. The pail is carried between them now.

They pass the picket-fenced gardens, bright with marigolds and petunias. Wooden decks and stairways, shutters and porches decorate the varied crowd of houses that people the main street of this narrow seaside town. The town has begun to awaken now.

Around the side of the house, a border of shells edges a brief strip of blossoms. In the door to the ground floor apartment, the rough lacework of macrame hangs against the pane, and Gabriel's hand releases the latch.

Piper says, "You haven't asked me my name."

"I have my own name for you."

Maybe Gabriel tells her, whispering, thrusting her fingers a second into the source of that frivolous appelation. Invites her to come in. More likely it's too soon. And she only says good-bye and disappears inside and

Piper is alone in the midmorning sunshine with the gray whelk shell in her hand.

Route 23: 10th and Bigler to Bethlehem Pike

Ain't no reason for you to be gaping at me. I pay my taxes, just like everybody else. And it just don't make no sense. The mayor and all them city council men sitting up in all them little offices over in City Hall, ain't never been cold in they life. And me and my little ones freezing to death up on Thirteenth Street.

Last time I was down to City Hall to try and talk to one of them men, heat just pouring out the radiator in that office. I had to yell at Kamitra and Junie not to touch it, scared they was gonna burn theyself. Man I'm talking to done took off his jacket and drape it over the back of his chair. Wiping his forehead off with his hanky, talking bout, "No, Miz Moses, we can't do nothing for you. Not a thing. Not as long as you living in a privately-own residence and you not in the public housing. . . ."

I'm thinking how they only use them offices in the day time. Ain't nobody in em at night. And my babies is sleeping in the kitchen, ever since the oil run out two weeks ago and they ain't deliver no more. Landlord claim he outta town.

Hasan, my baby here, he don't hardly even know what warm is. He so little he can't remember last summer. All the others done had colds all winter. Noses ain't stopped running since last October. And Kleenex just one more thing I can't afford to buy em. Scuse me a minute.

—I know, Junie. I see it. Yeah, I see the swings. Can't get off and play today. Too cold out there. Maybe so, honey. Maybe tomorrow, if the sun come out. Lamont, let your sister have a turn to sit by the window now.—

Don't you be thinking I'm homeless, cause I ain't. You ever see a bag lady with all these kids? These here shopping bags is just a temporary measure. Like I said, I live up on Thirteenth Street. Seventeen hundred block. North. Top floor. You don't believe me you go look. My name on the mailbox: Leona Mae Moses. And all the rest of the stuff belong to us is right where we left it. The kids is got other clothes, and we got beds and dishes and all the same stuff you got in your house. We ain't planning to make this no permanent way of life. Just till this cold spell break.

— Cherise, honey, would you get the baby bottle out that bag you got up there? Right next to that box of Pampers. And you and Lamont gonna have to get off and get some more milk. Next time we come up to the A & P. Junie, get your hands away from that buzzer. We ain't there yet. We got to go all the way up to Chestnut Hill, and then turn around and come back down. Anyway, it's Kamitra turn to ring the bell this time.—

Ain't nobody got no call to stare at me like I'm some kinda freak. My kids got the same rights as other people kids. They got a right to spend the night someplace warm and dry. Got a right to get some sleep at night. Last night, along about eleven o'clock, when the man on the radio say the temperature gone down to fifteen below, he didn't have to tell me nothing. The pipes is froze, and the wind lifting the curtains right up at the windows in my kitchen. And my little girl crying, "Mama, I'm cold." Air so icy I can see a little cloud come out her mouth, every time she cry.

— Kamitra, sugar, don't sing so loud. Mama trying to talk. Anyway, other people on here besides us. They don't want to be bother listen to all that racket.—

You got kids? Well, think a minute what you would do if you was in my place. Last night I'm trying so hard to think what to do, feel like my head gonna split wide open. Nobody in my building ain't got no more heat than we do. I don't know no neighbors got space enough for all of us. They be sleep anyway. All my people still down south.

Kamitra crying done waked up the others, too. Then all of em crying they cold. I ain't crazy yet, but I like to went crazy last night trying to think what I'm gonna do. I just kept thinking theys got to be some place in this great big city that I can carry these children to, where it's warm, where it stay warm, even in the middle of the night. And then it come to me.

"Mama, where we going?" the kids is all asking. I just tell em to hush and go get they blankets and towels and sweaters and stuff. Comb everybody hair and dress em real warm. Start packing up some food to last us for a couple days. "Mama, what we gonna do? Where we taking all this stuff?" And Junie, he tickle me. Say, "Mama, we can't go no place. It's dark outside."

I just hush em all up and hustle em down to the corner. Little ones start crying again, cause even with all them layers on, they ain't warm enough for no fifteen below. Lamont done lost his gloves last week, and Cherise just got one a my scarf wrap around her head, cause it ain't enough hats to go round. Ain't a one of em got boots. Cherise still asking me where we going, while we standing at the corner, waiting. I tell em, "Mama got a surprise for you all. We taking a trip. We going on a nice, long ride."

—Get outta that bag, Kamitra. You can't have no more crackers. Mama gonna fix you some tuna fish for supper, pretty soon. What's the matter Junie? You gotta pee? You sure? Well then, sit still. Lamont, next time we come up to our corner, I want you to take him in to the bathroom, anyway. It don't hurt to try.—

I guess that explain howcome we here. We intend to stay here, too, right where we at, up till the weather break. Or the oil come. Whatever happen first. It ain't no laws against it. I pay my taxes to keep these things running, just like everybody else. And I done paid our fare. The ones under six rides for free, just like the sign say. I got enough quarters here to last us a long time.

My kids is clean—all got washed up at the library just this morning. And look how nice and well-behave they is. I ain't got nothing to be ashamed of.

I hope your curiosity satisfied, cause I really ain't got no more to say. This car big enough for all of us. You better find something else to gawk at. Better look on out the window, make sure you ain't miss your stop.

—Cherise, sugar, we at the end of the line again. Go up there and put these quarters in the man box. No, Junie. This trolley gonna keep running all night long. Time just come for the man to turn the thing around. We ain't getting off. This trip ain't over yet.

Both Ways

Thursday:
I've made it here, all the way to the cabin I'll be staying in, and I'm sitting on the mattress I claimed and pulled under the window, with my backpack and sleeping bag dumped at the foot. The cabin is all wood, outside and in. Dusty floors, corners cobwebby. A long-legged spider headed up the wall, toward the window screen. The whole place smells of the country—sunshine, mildew, new mown grass. That rustic, earthy smell of places you can't shut up so tightly that you shut the outdoors out. My lap full of sunshine.

I'm here, at The Weekend, alone for the first time, this year. It isn't my fault I'm here alone. It's Maria's. She was the one who decided not to come.

As soon as I got in, Diana came running up shouting, "Corey and Maria are here!" And then, when she saw it was only me, didn't miss a beat. Shouted just as loud, "Hey, Corey! Good to see you! Where's Maria?"

So I got to explain casually to everybody in earshot that, yes, Maria and I are still together, that it's just because of the work for her classes this summer she decided not to come. And watch all their faces lapse into relief.

Diana looks good, already stripped down to country minimum: short short shorts, halter top, bare feet, her hair in cool summer cornrows. Last summer, she'd just broken up with her lover and she was a wreck. Looks like she's gained back all the weight she lost. In comparison, I know I look washed out and anemic. I haven't been out in the sun at all—too pale skin against too red eyebrows and lashes. Someone actually told me last week that the color of my hair made her hot to look at. Well, it's making me hot, too—and it'll probably take me an hour to find a barette.

Diana helped me carry my stuff over here and we got to talk a little. Asked her how it's been. "Good," she said. Said she's been taking her choreography much more seriously. "That's one thing that's easier," she said, "since Jan and I split up. I have a whole lot more time for dance. I've been coming up with new ideas so fast I hardly have time to work them up."

She looked really happy, practically radiant, and I couldn't help saying so. "You sound like you've finally gotten your life to be exactly the way you want it."

She smiled. "It took me awhile to get here. I had a whole lot of personal work to do."

Personal work. What does it mean? When I tried to tell Diana what *I've* been doing this past year, every sentence seemed to start with "We." Yet, when Maria decided she wasn't coming, I was excited. Wanted to come, even more, so I could be alone.

I told Diana that, and she said, "What? Are you crazy? You came *here* to be alone? A place where you'll be surrounded by a hundred other women, twenty-four hours a day, where they've got workshops and activities scheduled from morning to night, where there's not even any privacy in the bathrooms—and *you* came so you could be *alone?*" We were both laughing. But I can be alone here in a way I never can, at home. Here, I'm a separate person.

When I stop writing and look up, I'm overwhelmed. Even out a window, I haven't seen this much of the sky in a long time.

Friday:

Today at lunch I stood in the doorway with a plate full of spaghetti and a mug of cold cider, surveying the empty spaces at the picnic tables on the porch. Realizing it's been so long since I made even the simplest decision without taking Maria into account. I'd be asking her, "Where do you want to sit?" or "Is this O.K.?" I stood in the doorway wondering, "Where do *I* want to sit?" and just savoring that question. Until Nancy K. called, "Come and sit with us, Corey, and tell us what you're smiling about." And I felt so *welcome!*

I want to not feel guilty for liking being here alone. For thinking about what *I* need.

At my table, we got into talking about lesbian culture, and whether artists ought to identify more with the arts community or with the lesbian community. Diana was there, and Nancy K. is a photographer, and there was another woman who's a writer. Then Misty said she thinks lesbian artists and writers have a responsibility to the community to present positive images, and everybody jumped on her. Five of us sat around talking until three o'clock in the afternoon. I never would have done that if Maria were here.

But it's not just talk I need. At the workshop I went to this morning (Kate's: "Can Lesbians Be Friends?"), I had just opened a folding chair and sat down in the circle when someone moved up behind me and put a gentle arm around my shoulder, the skin soft and warm against mine. It was Marianne—she just wanted me to move over, so she could fit her chair in, too. But it shocked me so much. Nobody ever does that, ever just touches me that way. Other women here do that with each other all the time. But not with me. I've always been Maria's Lover.

What I'm feeling—relief? Relief that I'm still here, I guess. That some core of me has lasted, stayed intact. I like it. Like myself. I know other people are liking me, too. Old friends. Karen and Elaine from New York are here. And Linda Rush. Olga and Susan Schneider from Baltimore. But there are lots of women I don't know, too.

I'm intrigued by the fact that there are women here I perceive as sexually attractive. There is a woman from D.C. here for the first time whose name is Patty Sarachild. She has dark curly hair and dark eyes, and her skin is olive, almost brown. She looks Mediterranean, somehow, or like she could be a gypsy. There's an easy looseness to the way her body moves, as though she's more at home in it than I'll ever be in mine. She seems very young. I'm intrigued by her.

Saturday:

The woman named Patty is taking up much more of my

thoughts than I'm comfortable with. In all the time I've been with Maria, I've never figured out how to reconcile feelings I might have for someone else. Beginning when I was very young—even younger than Patty probably is now—I used to fall in love with different women (girls, really) all the time. I developed complex crushes, fascinations, obsessions. I tried to convince myself I had come to the end of that phase when I met Maria.

I don't know exactly what these feeling are that I seem to be developing for Patty. I don't believe it's a crush—but would I admit it if it were? I'm just engaged by her, taken in. Keep watching her.

She's been flirting with practically every woman here. Outrageously, sometimes dangerously, like with Karen while Elaine is right in the next room moving chairs. Maybe she doesn't know they're a couple. Or maybe she doesn't care. But acting that way seems flagrant and volatile here. She's out of context. Where does she belong?

I can imagine her in some kind of old-fashioned Italian comedy—cast as a stock player like Harlequin and Columbine and the others. She'd be a rogue: Petronella. Or she could be a wicked little girl in a French art film, who wears rouge and lipstick before she's old enough, and runs away with a lover three times her age. She has the body of a fifteen-year-old kid, and her face and mouth are young, too. Her eyes could be thirty.

This morning, she and I were both in Elaine's workshop ("Ethics and Relationships"), sitting directly across from one another. I looked up and she was watching me. I looked away, at other women, at Elaine, listened to the discussion, even made a comment, and then later I looked back, and Patty Sarachild was right where I'd left her, still with her eyes on me—pinning the moment down before I could look away again, fastening something between us, now, that we'd have to reckon with. Smiling. It wasn't until I smiled back that it finally hit me that now she was flirting with me.

After the break in the middle of the workshop, she didn't take the same chair she'd had before, but the one I was leaning against, where I was sitting on the floor. Sat in it with one leg hanging over touching me, from my shoulder all the way down my side. It was all I was aware of for the next whole hour.

Tactfully, gracefully, casually, accidentally—I couldn't figure out how to move away. It seemed absurd to, when all around the room other women were leaning against each other, holding hands, gently massaging someone's shoulders. Including women who are not lovers with each other. It's what women always do here.

So I plunged into the discussion, the next opening that came along. I don't even remember what I said, but I must've used Maria's name about twenty times. And Patty went right on sitting with her leg against my side, carrying on in the discussion as if nothing were happening, and using the word lover only in plural, as if she'd had hundreds.

*

Mid-afternoon, and I've finally gotten away—far away from everybody. I found a dirt road that looked abandoned, followed it way back through the wood. It came out in this lovely meadow. Waist-high grass and acres and acres of sky. Everything hot—still—suspended. I saw a redwing blackbird and a blue, blue butterfly. Found droppings and tracks from a deer. On the road here I found a jay's feather. I put it between the pages of this journal to save for Maria. One of the blues is the same shade as her eyes. She'll run her forefinger across the edge, and maybe put it in her hair. I'm longing to see her again, talk to her about all I've been thinking, about being separate and what my needs are.

Right now I have exactly what I need—time out to be alone in this lovely lush meadow. I want to stay here for hours, letting the sun slow me down—stay nested in this hollow of green with the grasses tall around me, letting the earth hold me and hush me until I feel strengthened and centered and ready to meet whatever comes next.

*

I met Patty Sarachild on the road back, walking the way I'd come.

Even though we have never actually talked about it, it's always been very clear between Maria and me what our expectations are of each other. I know she will never go off pursuing another woman, as long as we're together, and she knows I never will. But what if another woman is pursuing me?

Of course, it was probably a coincidence that Patty chose to take the same walk I did, the same afternoon. But instead of going on, she turned around and said she'd walk with me. What she said was, "I just wondered where this road went. But if you've already been there you can tell me. I don't need to find out for myself." Now I wonder if she meant more by that than I heard at first.

I asked her questions about herself. Encountered a lot of blanks. She read about The Weekend in *off our backs*. Got a ride here with Kate and Donna, but had only met them once before. Doesn't have a career, or even a job. Didn't go to college. Has lived in D.C. for seven months (in four places, so far), and is thinking about leaving, but doesn't know where she wants to go. The woman is an unknown quantity.

When I stopped, frustrated, she turned to me and said, "Now I get to ask you questions." And launched into, "When did you first come out? Who with? What was it like, the first time? Did you have an orgasm?" Then, when I blushed and started to stammer, she used that as an excuse to touch me, saying, "It's O.K. You don't have to answer that." Leaving my flesh flaming like a kiss.

We were quiet, walking side by side, until we were almost back. Then, out of the blue, she told me she's been out since she was thirteen. That she spent her adolescence in homes for girls and reform schools. For running away. That her mother was an alcoholic, and is dead now. Patty is twenty.

I don't know why she told me those things. Can she know that hers is the kind of story that I've such a weakness for, the kind that is far too easy for me to romanticize?

Does there have to be a reason, a purpose behind what she told me? Why do I feel as though she must be after something? And does it really happen, anyway, that out of nowhere some woman comes pursuing you? What kind of signals have *I* been sending out?

Tonight at dinner, Diana and I sat with Donna and Kate and some of the other women from D.C. And I asked them about Patty. I had a suspicion it might be good for me to hear what they had to say. They said things like, "Isn't she too much?" and "She's a bit intense, isn't she?" Donna said, "Yeah, she came with us, but your guess is as good as mine who she'll go home with." Marianne said, "She's cute. But she's such a kid. If I were twenty years younger, though. . . ."

They laughed a lot, as if Patty were an in-family joke among them, but affectionately, as if she were a child who'd just reached a perverse but entertaining stage that must be simply tolerated by the surrounding adults. But Diana said, "Patty's a heartbreaker, already. There must be women hurting for her scattered all up and down the East Coast." She wasn't laughing when she said it. Diana is not from D.C.

Marianne said, "Come on, Di, you don't mean Patty's got a reputation all the way to Boston."

"She used to live in Boston," Diana said. "And I think she'd have a hard time finding friends if she ever tried to come back."

So I suppose I have been warned. Did I need warning?

Of all the bizarre things, a line from the Ten Commandments flashes into my mind. "Thou shalt not covet thy neighbor's wife. . . ." It makes me laugh. Patty is hardly anybody's wife. But I know why it came to me. When I was a kid, after I learned what "covet" meant, I always used to wonder how you could *not* covet. How could you will yourself not to want things? How could you just slam a hold on your desires and prevent them from happening, lock a ball and chain on your fantasies and keep them from running away? I still don't know.

"Cheating." An ugly word. Radclyffe Hall cheated on Una Troubridge and Una forgave her. Wouldn't even use that word—I think she called them "transgressions" or "indiscretions" or something. Of course, those two had a double standard. But it worked for them, twenty-eight years—until Radclyffe died.

I have never cheated at anything. I've always played fair, been honest on exams, on job interviews. . . . The week after my twelfth birthday, I went to the Saturday matinee and lied about my age, to get in for half price. I felt so guilty I had to write a letter to the movie theater, sending them the other half dollar.

Is it cheating on Maria to look at Patty and to like her dark eyes and dark curls, and her Mediterranean coloring? Was it cheating to smile back when she smiled at me? Is it cheating to *like* the thought that maybe she followed me? Am I cheating by writing about her here? I suppose I should be talking to somebody, like Diana, about this. Asking these questions out loud. I don't want to. It's hard enough to write them. And anyway, then I'd have to listen to the answers.

What throws me about all of this is that I love Maria. I can close my eyes and immediately see her face—when she's just taken her glasses off, and I'm struck again by the startling intensity of her blue eyes. When she wants to make love, her smile coy with seductiveness, her fingers very slowly undoing her buttons while her eyes never leave my face. Or when we are making love, her features soft and indistinct, her black hair in a tangle all over the pillow, and us in a tangle too, damp and delectable. I want to go on loving her for years and years. And I don't want to do anything that might make her stop loving me. . . .

The way I'm feeling about Patty doesn't have anything to do with me and Maria. It couldn't come anywhere near it. So how could it possibly threaten that love? If I appreciate Patty, that doesn't diminish my love for Maria, steal anything that should rightfully be hers.

Then why do I feel guilty? I've hardly done anything except think, and I feel guilty as hell. Or maybe it's what I *haven't* done. I haven't ignored her. I haven't rebuffed her. I haven't dismissed her from my thoughts. But why should I? I want to feel relaxed about this, even righteous. To feel clear and strong and good about my right to appreciate whomever I please. To know that, whatever Maria might fear (if she knew), this isn't going to hurt her. Or hurt "us." Why do I feel so defensive?

I've just read this entry over. "Appreciate." What a very careful word to choose. What is it I really mean, and am afraid to write, even here? I say I have always been honest, but am I being honest with myself?

Sunday:

This morning, woke up at dawn to a hundred birds singing and a blanket of wet mist smothering the flat field. Everything saturated with dew. Diana and I were going to watch the sunrise. But the sky is gray and full of clouds, and when I went to wake her, she said she'd rather sleep. I've come back to the meadow by myself. This is the last day.

Last night was clear and much warmer than the other nights. After I finished writing out all those thoughts, I took my sleeping bag and found a place to sleep outside. This time I know she followed me. Patty. She came up and asked if she could join me for a while, and sat down on the other end of my sleeping bag.

The moon was nearly full, and so bright that it threw long shadows of the two of us across the grass. The whole place was quiet. We both sat there without saying anything, with only the sound of cicadas and a nightjar somewhere off in the wood. I wasn't watching her, but I could tell she was looking at me. That same thing was between us that she'd secured there early in the morning, which seemed like years ago.

I tried to think of something casual and friendly to say. My mouth felt like a dry creek bed, where nothing has flowed for years. I sat frozen at my end of the sleeping bag, hugging my knees to my chest, and keeping my eyes on her shadow on the grass. It sprawled there, just a few feet away from my shadow, looking long and lopsided but totally at ease. The nightjar stopped and a cricket swelled, very shrill, right near my foot. Then it stopped, too.

"Corey," she said. "You're pretty."

The words splashed over me like an unexpected shower, a cloudburst on a hot summer night. Spilled through me, drenching every fiber suddenly awake, alert to exactly what this thing between us was. It was not just her, flirting with me. It was my mouth that was dry, my arms that were wrapped around me tight as an overwound spring. My skin had burst into flame when she'd touched me before, and now was aflame all over, my heart lurching, falling, and turning over and over in its fall.

Words came spewing out. "Listen, Patty." I said it very fast, not to give her a chance to break in. "I have to tell you about Maria. My lover. I don't know if you were listening or not, in the workshop yesterday, but she's the one I was talking about, that I've been together with for six years. And I love her. I mean, we love each other. I mean, maybe you don't believe in long-term relationships, but we still do. That's the way we've chosen to live our life."

I enumerated all the details. How we met, at one of these Weekends, but didn't just jump into bed with each other right then and there, how it took us months to become lovers. How we'd go places separately, and then walk each other home. Write letters back and forth across town, and call each other up two or three times a day. I told her how we were lovers for two years before we lived together, and that now we've been living together for four years.

She didn't say anything.

I told her that Maria and I bought a house together, and I told her how much trouble and time and money we've taken to fix it up. I went into minute descriptions of stripping the woodwork and sanding the floors and installing the fiberglass insulation on the basement ceiling.

She sat there watching me with her body relaxed into that disarming frankness. It was too dark to tell what was on her face. She still didn't say anything, so I told her that Maria and I intend to stay together, that we aren't about to let anything, or anyone come between us. I told her we don't believe in breaking our commitments to each other. I told her we don't believe in non-monogamy.

And then she finally said something. She said, "What are you afraid of?"

I couldn't believe it. I just laced into her. "I don't know who you think you are, but there're a few things you'd better learn, before you grow up. You can't just go sauntering through your life, and whenever you see something you think you want, just take it. This kind of love I'm talking is serious! It's forever! It's not just something you take off and hang up over night, and then put back on again in the morning. Yeah, the choices you make rule out a lot of other chances. But you stay with those choices. Because you can't have it both ways."

She looked subdued. She looked like a sullen schoolgirl just caught breaking the dormitory rules. I felt like a lecturing housemother. It suddenly seemed absurd. Because I'm the one who has to live by the rules—clearly they don't matter a bit to her.

She wasn't looking at me any more. She was gathering herself up to go. "O.K.," she said. "I hear you." And then, "Goodnight."

I watched her slight figure amble across the moonlit field, away from me. Then I crawled into the sleeping bag by myself. The paradigm of morality. Knowing I'd done the right thing, the only thing, and wondering why I couldn't have kept my mouth shut.

Now, this cloudy morning in the wet meadow, I feel awful. This is crazy. I'm grieving for something that surely I'm better off without. What could I possibly have gotten out of it? One night together that would feel like larceny—that I'd be paying back with guilt for years? A reckless, spontaneous weekend and the rest of my life in ruins?

Patty Sarachild. I won't be another broken heart on your string.

Oh, hell. They're ringing the bell for breakfast already. I'll have to run all the way back.

*

Spent the whole morning doing evaluations and plans for next year, and then clean-up. I didn't see Patty at all. She didn't show up for evaluation. At lunch, when everyone was saying goodbyes, she was signed up for kitchen shift. Did she do that to avoid people, or to make them seek her out? All through lunch I thought I would leave without talking to her again. Ended up seeking her out.

For a minute or two, she acted as if nothing had happened last night. Turned around from the sink, laughing and playing, threatening to hug me with soap suds all the way up to her elbows. Of course, there were other women in the kitchen, laughing and joking, too. And I thought: it was a mistake to come in here. Then she wiped off the soapsuds and really did hug me, and kissed me, and said very softly, just under my ear, "I still think you're pretty."

*

Diana drove me to the bus. "I don't know where the weekend went," she said. "I thought we'd get lots more time to talk."

"Yeah, me too," I said. "I'm sorry. I guess I was kind of preoccupied."

I watched her for a minute. After four days in the sun, her skin seemed burnished, glowing. The wind coming in the window rippled the ruffles on her sundress (clearly chosen for a return to civilization). Everything else about her was still—the careful braids on her head, the silver loops in her ears, her face in a reverie. I took a chance.

"Tell me," I said. "What do you know about Patty Sarachild?" Diana's whole face changed. But now I had to go on. "The other night, when you said what you did about her being such a—"

I was going to say "heartbreaker," but Diana finished it off with "homewrecker?"

"Well, yeah. How do you know? You weren't . . ."

"Involved with her? Uh-uh." She shook her head and set the earrings swinging. Another car coming from The Weekend passed us, honking and everyone waving. When it was gone, she said, "It was Jan—my ex."

"Oh, Diana," I said, and didn't know what else to say. Finally I asked, "Was it hard for you to have to be around her all weekend?"

"She knew enough to keep her distance." Diana sighed and sent a shrug rolling off her shoulders down her back. "Anyway, it's hardly a live issue any more." Then she changed the subject. "Look, Corey," she said, glancing across at me, "are you sure things are all right between you and Maria?"

"They were when I left," I said. She shot me another look, sharp with disbelief. And I looked down in my lap. This business about honesty again. All right. "I don't know," I said.

Now I'm on the bus, my handwriting full of loops and jags from every rut and pothole on the highway. I'm on my way home. To Maria. My Lover.

So what was this all about: Patty Sarachild? What in the world was going on?

The word that comes to me is "affair." But that's preposterous. We never did anything. And won't. I don't need those complications in my life. Can't it be enough that she liked me, was attracted to me, saw me as someone loveable—or whatever the hell was going on. That's all I wanted—to be flattered and flirted with, intrigued and charmed. I'll admit it: I loved it. But that was enough of it. I know when to stop.

Only I'm not ready to. Not yet. What do I do with all these left-over feelings? That tension that pulled between us, walking side by side through the woods, just an arm's reach apart. No sound but the twigs snapping under our feet. A scoop of her olive back in the neck of her shirt. Feeling drenched in her, in her presence. That place on my arm where she touched me—a patch of fire. And then, this morning, that kiss . . .

We just turned off the highway. I need to stop. I need to think about Maria. Maybe she'll be at the station. I told her what time the bus got in—if she didn't lose the scrap of paper she wrote it on—if she didn't get swamped at the library.

I'll stop in another minute. When we turn into State Street. But I just want to write one more time what Patty said to me. Get it down while I'm still close to it, can remember exactly how her voice sounded, soft and cajoling in the summer night.

"You're pretty." She said that. No one else besides Maria has ever thought I was pretty. I want to remember.

And I wish I could forget the other thing she said, in the field, in the dark, her voice ringing out, clear and daring.

What are you afraid of?

Her Ex-Lover

I can see when I turn the corner onto Second Street that Ernestine is waiting for me. I catch a glimpse of her every few feet as I make my way up the crowded block. She's in the blue slacks she pressed last night, her brown arms bare in a light striped summer shirt. The shirt is loose, hanging out over her slacks. She always wears her shirts that way—I think from some self-consciousness about her size. Ernestine is much more solid than me, but she's taller too, and I think she looks fine the size she is.

She's sitting in a patch of sunlight at the top of the five stone steps that lead up to the travel agency and on into our apartment building. In the spotlight of sun her skin is golden brown, and the full circle of her hair is a brilliant bronze flame. I want to surprise her, to come up quietly behind, lean against her broad back and stretch my arms around her. I love coming home to Ernestine—to lock our door upstairs and get lost in her hugs and kisses, and then to hear all about her morning.

She hasn't seen me coming because of the dozens of people jamming the sidewalk. In the middle of a weekday, our block is a zoo. Twelve-fifteen and all the office workers have been let out for their noontime feeding—including us. But that's why we chose to live downtown, imagining what a relief it would be to come home in the middle of a working day and just be ourselves for half an hour. . . .

As I reach our stoop, I see there's another reason Ernestine didn't spot me coming. There's someone with her, sitting beside her on the white stone steps, and the two of them are talking. I'm close enough now to see who it is. Lisa. Her last lover. Her white lover.

Lisa looks up and sees me coming first, and she says, "Hi, Shirley," with a smile that doesn't look for real.

"Hi, Lisa. Ernie."

Ernie flashes me a swift, silent apology, and gets up to give me a brief, respectable kiss.

"Did the mail come yet?"

"I didn't look," Ernie says, and I get to escape for a minute, ducking into the vestibule to check our box. There's only a circular from some sweepstakes, and another with some grinning sap running for city council. By the time I'm back to Ernestine and Lisa on the steps, they aren't talking anymore, and when Ernestine begins again, it's to start explaining things to me.

"You know how Lisa's been planning to move out to California?"

Most of the time, I would just as soon not know what Lisa is planning. But Ernestine has been keeping me posted on this for weeks. Lisa quit her job. Lisa gave notice on her apartment. Two Sundays ago, we went to a porch sale Lisa had, where Ernie actually paid her for a radio that used to belong to both of them. Lisa could probably use the money—for her trip.

"Yeah, sure."

"Well, today is the big day. She's taking off this afternoon."

Lisa chimes in with, "Finally! Huh, Shirley?" She's only half teasing. Lisa knows how I feel about her. Her pale gray eyes watch me for a second, from under the fringe of blond hair. Maybe she expects me to protest politely that she shouldn't put it like that. I haven't got a thing to say.

But Lisa's never at a loss for conversation. She goes chattering on, "I can hardly believe I'm really leaving for good."

I can hardly believe it either. For good! My luck doesn't usually run that way.

"Yesterday, I went down and closed out my checking account at Mutual. I've had an account there for almost ten years. It felt so—final. And then this morning, when I was cleaning out the refrigerator and packing the last few things—you know, my toothbrush and towel and stuff—I started feeling like I was watching myself in a movie or something. It didn't seem real."

"It's a big change to make," Ernie says. "Even if you have been planning it for months."

"Seems like years."

It does seem like years. Because ever since Lisa started saying she was leaving town, she's gotten more and more important to Ernestine.

Last Friday morning we were both in the kitchen—me stirring the grits on the stove, and Ernie walking back and forth putting together lunches, even more quiet than she usually is.

"Shirley?"

I looked over, but she wasn't looking at me—paying a lot of attention to tearing off the lengths of wax paper just so. "Yeah?"

"I wanted to tell you that I made some plans for tomorrow night." She looked up, and my surprise must have been right across my face. We always check in with the other first, before we make a commitment for both of us to do anything. "There wasn't something else we were supposed to do, was there?" she asked.

"Nothing special." I waited for her to go on, but Ernestine never says more than she has to. "What kind of plans did you make?"

She rattled the drawer open and started to rummage for a knife. "With Lisa. We're going out to dinner, and then spend one last evening together."

"All three of us?" I never knew which was worse—being with the two of them together, or being alone, and knowing that they were together somewhere anyway, without me.

Now it was Ernie surprised. She stopped right where she was— standing bent over to one side with her arms up to the elbows in the utensil drawer. "I guess I just automatically assumed you wouldn't be interested."

"In other words, I'm not invited." I couldn't keep the meanness out of my voice. "After all, it's only Saturday night."

"Shirley." Her voice only sounded a trifle impatient, but her hands jerked so quickly the drawer banged shut. "Don't you think it might be good for both of us—for all three of us—if Lisa and I just had one good long final talk? Just to clarify things once and for all."

Ernestine had already started to cut up the cucumber, as if whatever I might answer wasn't going to make much difference. Her hands had found their calmness again, and she stood there, solid and impenetrable, slicing off crisp, thin, even circles. Next to her, everything else looked small—the tiny knife in her broad, sure fist, the little squares of sandwiches, the narrow space between the table and the counter that she nearly filled. I could feel the rage rising in me. "I don't understand! I just do not understand what it is you all have so much to say about. What do you do—reminisce about the good old days when she used to treat you like a half-wit and you used to let her?"

Half to herself, she said, "Maybe I never should have told you anything about it." And then, laying down the knife and turning to me, "Look. The woman is leaving town next week. It may be years before I see her again. Maybe never. The least I can do is take her out to dinner."

"You're *taking* her to dinner?"

Neither one of us noticed the rank gray clouds of smoke from the grits on the stove. The pot was scorched beyond saving. We didn't make up for two days.

"You know, Shirley, I'm glad you came home." Lisa is after my attention again. "I wasn't sure if I'd see you or not. Ernestine said sometimes you get rush jobs you have to finish and you can't take your lunch break on time. But I wanted to say goodbye to you both."

To us both. I sit leaning against the railing, meeting that unflinching gaze, not knowing what to say. I'm still thinking about that fight, and so many others Ernestine and I have had because of this woman. Who is supposed to be Ernestine's *ex*-lover, but who has just never made her graceful exit off this stage. Claiming some crazy notion that she considers "liberated," about how healthy it is for former lovers to remain friends. I'm thinking about how much I have resented her, how many times I've wished she didn't exist, or could somehow just vanish. Why does she want to say goodbye to me when she's never been my friend?

Not that she didn't try. I guess she saw, as soon as Ernie and I took up with each other, that the only way she could keep from losing Ernestine altogether was to try to be friends with me, too. So she started cultivating a whole new set of interests she thought I could relate to.

The first year Ernie and I were together, Lisa showed up at our place on my birthday with a present for me, all wrapped up in gold paper and curly ribbons. I didn't know what to say. All I could think was that I was not about to start buying this white girl birthday presents. She was hanging over me with an excited look on her face like she'd just brought me something she knew I'd wanted all my life but could never afford. "Open it, Shirley."

"Yeah, go ahead." Ernestine was trying to make it seem perfectly natural. "Open it."

I opened it. It was a copy of *Their Eyes Were Watching God*.

I've never had much tact in situations like that, and Lisa could pick it up. "Don't you like Zora Neale Hurston?"

I love Zora Neale Hurston. I've read everything she ever wrote—that's in print. I shifted the book from one hand to the other, not knowing what to do with it. "I already have a copy," I said.

Lisa, of course, looked hurt. One of the things she's an expert at.

Ernestine asked her what she thought of Hurston's book. And it turned out that Lisa hadn't read it herself. So I ended up giving it back to her and sending her home to read it. I didn't really expect her to.

But she finished it and went on to Nella Larsen, and then Ann Petry, and after that Alice Walker. She came back wanting to discuss them all with me. And that was only the beginning. She studied up on black history, and started listening to jazz. She went to some CR groups or something they were having for white women on confronting their own racism. She even started taking dancing lessons. Stuff she never did for Ernestine when they were together.

When they *were* together, it was always Lisa's culture that mattered. Lisa was always making Ernie feel like she didn't even *have* any culture—dragging her around to "openings" and French restaurants all the time, and trying to talk her into going back to school. Nothing about Ernestine was good enough then.

Once, when Ernestine and I first started going together, we were getting ready to go to a party, and I asked her what kind of places she and Lisa used to go to.

She shrugged her shoulders, turning to the closet to hunt for the scarf she wanted to wear. "We went to museums and stuff a lot. Concerts."

"What kind of concerts?" At that time, Lisa hadn't developed her taste for jazz yet.

Ernie tied a peacock blue scarf several different ways before the mirror. She answered casually, "We went to hear the symphony orchestra a lot. And sometimes at one of the art galleries we'd go hear a woodwind ensemble or a string quartet or something like that."

Even the words sounded phony in Ernestine's mouth. I could picture her, clapping politely after every charming little étude, making small talk during the intermissions, and "mingling" about as naturally as a Saint Bernard in a pen full of Pekingese.

It made me smolder—even the little bit she would tell to answer my questions. Because I knew Lisa never appreciated Ernie, never understood how special she is, or how much Ernie loved her, never realized how much *she* was getting out of being with Ernie, that it wasn't just a one-way street. Not until they split.

Ernestine finally left her, but Lisa never gave Ernie up. . . .

"I heard New Mexico's supposed to be beautiful, too. Shirley's sister was there on vacation last year, and she said she fell in love with it."

Hearing my name brings my mind back to this afternoon. Ernestine, true to her Libra nature, has been filling in the awkward spaces with words, trying to cover up for my own silence.

"Maybe I'll stop there for a couple of days on my way across," Lisa says. But there's only so much two people can say about places neither one of them's ever been. So the conversation fizzles out again.

The three of us are clumped uncomfortably on the steps, and now they're both looking at me. I can see Ernestine trying to assess what I'm thinking, how I'm feeling.

All of a sudden, I stand up. I need to move. "Did you eat yet?" I ask Ernestine.

"Not yet."

"Would you like—"

"Do you want—" we've both turned to Lisa.

"No thanks," she says. "I just got finished with breakfast. I'll stop for something later, on the road."

"Then I'll just go up and get our lunches," I say. "I have to be back at work by one."

When I start up the steps, Ernestine says, "Shirley?"

"Yeah?"

"Lisa brought over some stuff she had left in her kitchen that she thought we might be able to use. It's on the table and on the counter—you'll see."

When I walk in, every square inch of surface space in the kitchen is crammed with jars and boxes, cans and packages. Soy meal. Alfalfa seeds. Brewer's yeast. Seaweed. Stuff we never use.

Castoffs. Lisa trying to shove these castoffs onto us, that have nothing to do with us, no place in our culture. Just the way she tried to shove them down Ernestine's throat all those years. And I think sometimes she views Ernestine as her castoff, like a dress you give to a good friend, expecting you'll be able to borrow it back if you ever want it again. She doesn't seem to remember it was Ernestine who was through with her.

Sometimes, I get furious with Ernestine for letting Lisa treat her the way she did. For not having more pride.

When Ernestine and I first met, Ernie was all I could think about day and night. But we weren't lovers right away. She was still so swamped with guilt over leaving Lisa, she hardly even noticed I was around. I knew she had Lisa on her mind all the time, and I never gave her any peace over it.

"Don't you know," I used to demand, "that no white person can really love you? That they're only in it for what they can get out of it? Out of you?"

More often than not, she wouldn't answer. Just listen in silence while I'd go on and on—an alert, sharp-eared silence that was a lot more unnerving than her disagreeing with me would have been.

"Don't you see," I'd insist, "why you love her, or think you love her? It's power you're in love with. Privilege. You don't want her. You want to *be* her."

Once she cut me short, asking, "Shirley, if I felt like that, would I bother with you?"

But I couldn't let it rest for a long time, even after I knew Ernie was interested in me. Whenever I found out she'd seen Lisa, or talked to her on the phone, I'd feel compelled to try to make her recognize the weakness she had to overcome. "Can't you understand," I challenged, "that as long as you still love her you're hating yourself? That when you finally come to love yourself, black will be the most beautiful to you?"

"Do you really believe that, Shirley?"

"Do I believe it? Of course I believe black is beautiful."

"No. What you said about me."

We were coming from the women's restaurant, at night, and we both stopped walking, faced each other, and I remember she put her hand on my arm. It was one of the first times she ever touched me, and when she looked into my face I felt like she could see through every slogan and scrap of rhetoric I'd ever spouted off.

"Do you really believe I hate myself?"

I finally came to see that there are things about Ernestine that I may never understand, that I'll never change. One of them is the way she can't help giving of herself to any person—woman or man, black or white, gay, straight—who is unhappy, or alone. Another is the way she looks hard for what she likes in people, and won't let the things she doesn't like keep her from loving them. That's what she did—with me.

There was never a winner in any of those arguments with Ernie. There still isn't—winner or loser. The one last weekend went on right through Friday, Friday night, and all day Saturday. And then, Saturday night, Ernestine went out with Lisa anyway. She was gone until one in the morning, and I didn't go anywhere. I stayed in the apartment, seething, cleaning out the drawers in my desk and plotting what I was going to say when she came in. But the second I heard her key in the lock, suddenly I didn't want to fight with her any longer. I don't know why.

We stayed a long time that night, just holding each other, and both of us were crying.

I find our lunches in the refrigerator, behind a huge container of cottage cheese that's taken up residence on the top shelf. Head back downstairs with them. Outside, I park myself on the steps again and hand Ernie her bag. She thanks me but doesn't open it, and I don't really feel hungry either.

I watch Lisa talking, watch the gestures she makes with her hands. Every time I have ever seen her, she's had something in her hands—proofs of her busy responsibilities—books, or keys, or the strap of a heavy bag braced against her shoulder. More often than not, it'll be something she wants to give one of us—a magazine with an article in it she wants me to read, or maybe some notepads her aunt gave her that she thought Ernie could use. But now she is empty-handed. Her two hands hover above her lap, fluttering like the matching wings of a butterfly.

"I've never really been anywhere," she's answering. "I've never been further west than Cincinnati. But I've been dreaming about California all my life. I want to see the giant redwoods and the cable cars." She laughs. "I want to see Shirley Temple's handprints in the sidewalk. . . ."

I watch the people passing on the street. Two young black women approach, chic in expensive hairdos and designer clothes, trying to hurry in the precarious shoes that complete the required outfit. I wonder what this hour holds for them—maybe rushing to get a prescription filled, or buy a kid some sneakers, maybe to cash a paycheck and still have time to grab a bite at Burger King.

"Anyway, I think change is good for you," Lisa explains. "And I haven't had enough of it. I've been in the same rut too long. . . ."

In a clot, three white businessmen saunter along, identical in gray, three-piece suits, getting some sun on a leisurely stroll to "The Club" where lunch will be charged to expense accounts. Their heads turn of one accord when the two women pass them by.

". . . But I guess the real reason is that I've finally realized I need to . . . cut myself loose."

I turn to watch Lisa again, and find her eyes on me—flickering with an uncertainty that draws me instantly closer than her most reassuring smile.

"I mean," she says, "the past is past." She shrugs her shoulders, opens her hands.

When she stands up, there seems to be somehow less of her than I've seen before. On the sidewalk, at the foot of the stairs, she looks little—frail. I've always seen her dressed well. But today she's wearing pants that are old and faded, and a gray sleeveless shirt hangs loose on her figure. Its edges are frayed. Her pale hair is wispy and hasn't been cut lately; in the bright sunlight, I can see that some of its strands are not, after all, blond but gray.

"Well, I guess this is it," she says.

"Listen, Lisa." My own voice catches me by surprise. "I hope you'll be happy." Suddenly, I do.

She hugs us both quickly. "I won't say goodbye," she says. We watch her down the block, a small gray figure that gets almost immediately absorbed into the crowd.

I can feel Ernestine looking at me, sideways, trying again to gauge my thoughts. She says, "Well, I guess you're glad that's over."

I guess I should be. But there's a sound underneath her voice that makes me turn to her, fills me up with unexpected remorse. I want to take her in my arms, but we're standing out on Second Street in broad daylight with a hundred people passing by. I say what I can. "I know how much you'll miss her."

Together we walk back toward Main Street. Slowly, silently. Not touching, as we'd like to be, but close.

Past Halfway

I

There was too much sky here. It was too blue. She felt set adrift across this continent, like a paper boat without a sail on a pond wider than anyone could ever reach across. Some wind at her back—some momentum—still sent her skimming, but how long could that last?

Now there was nothing distinct before her, no clear goal Jo-Ellen could watch approaching. Just that long tape of road unrolling into infinity, dividing the flat, barren land in two identical halves. It was early summer and the day was unbearably bright. She was sealed under the bright dome of sky like an insect under a glass jar. Only the Volkswagen sheltered her. The hard green shell of the car was her carapace. In it, she carried everything she thought she might need to get on with the rest of her life.

She had left the books with Deborah. The dishes, the sewing machine—all the household stuff. Jo-Ellen took the car. It had not been planned like that. They had always imagined that they would divide things fairly—back in the days when they had not seriously imagined they would ever break up. But by the time that happened, it had been too long since anything was fair between them. Life wasn't fair. She had moved out—temporarily, she thought—months ago, staying with friends, then subletting a room in a communal house, and finally living at the residence hall of the YWCA—the most depressing of all. The times she spent at Deborah's became more and more like visits—tense, strained times when eventually she felt like she had to ask before making herself a cup of coffee—in a flat that was still filled with things that had belonged to both of them, the same flat that had been her home for five years.

"You still don't want me around, do you?" she had said, finally, during what turned out to be the last of those visits.

"I never said I didn't want you around, Jo-Ellen," Deborah had answered. She had folded her arms across her chest, her hands hidden in the folds of the big bulky sweater she was wearing, and leaned toward Jo-Ellen across the kitchen table. Her face, suddenly very close, seemed colorless, starkly pale against the black hair that was pulled back into a loose braid. Her dark eyes were bright and sharp. "You always think of everything in terms of yourself." Her voice sounded tired. "All I said was that I wanted to go to Toronto for the weekend." Now the voice was slowing to a painstaking pace, but rising in pitch. "What that means is, I want to *be* in Toronto for the *weekend*. It doesn't have anything to do with you."

"But you wouldn't let me come along, would you?"

Deborah pushed back her chair with sudden force and sprang to her feet. "For God's sake, Jo-Ellen! Why should I? I told you I'm going to visit Judy. You don't even know her. I told you she just got separated from her husband, and she wants to talk. We'll probably talk about her stupid *husband* the whole time! You'd be bored out of your mind."

Jo-Ellen stared up at Deborah. The familiar features were rigid with anger that Jo-Ellen's own temper was rising to meet. "You always have some excuse," she spurted. "There's always some emergency, or someone you can't disappoint. For the past two months it's been somebody every weekend. You don't seem to care about disappointing me."

Deborah opened her mouth to reply, but Jo-Ellen wouldn't let her. "I thought if I moved out for awhile, the whole thing would change. I figured you'd have lots of time all week long to do the stuff you want to do, and see everybody else. I thought maybe you'd miss me a little. But you don't even want to see me on the weekends any more." He voice began to quaver, and she broke off. She pressed her forehead against the knot of her clasped hands, propped on her elbows on the table. The words that came out were not really for Deborah. "You *are* avoiding me. You don't want to have anything to do with me any more."

Deborah sank into the chair across from her again. It was a long time before she spoke. Finally she expelled a long sigh. "All right, Jo-Ellen. I guess you're right—I guess I have been avoiding you. I just don't want—this—any more. Every time I see you you're miserable. Every time we get together we have to talk about our 'problem.' Well, maybe I don't have a problem. Maybe it's *your* problem. And maybe it's time to talk to somebody else about it besides me. When was the last time you made a friend?"

She paused for a second. When Jo-Ellen didn't answer, she went on. "When was the last time you belonged to a group that was doing anything worthwhile? Or even something just for fun? What about that course in layout you said you were going to take? What happened with that? You never even went to the first class."

Jo-Ellen was silent. She had no defenses against Deborah's attack, against the deep lines that ridged Deborah's forehead and drew her dark brows together, against her accusing eyes. A single lock of hair had escaped from the confines of the braid to curl beside Deborah's cheek, and Jo-Ellen fixed on it, watching it bounce and shake to match the vehemence in Deborah's voice, emphasizing every word. Deborah's voice had risen again.

"And so you moved out. What does that prove? Every time you come here, it's just the same as it always was. It's worse. I feel like I'm on probation. I can feel you trying to calculate whether I've had enough freedom to want to live with you again. Well, I don't want to live with you, if every time I go up to Toronto I have to ask your permission first. Not if every time I call up Margie, or my brother invites me to go camping with them, or the Jewish women's group has a potluck, I have to feel guilty. I'm tired of always feeling like you're reproaching me. I'm allowed to have friends, Jo-Ellen. I'm allowed to care about people other than you."

"You *don't* care about me."

The charge reverberated in the room as Deborah was finally silent. When she spoke again, her voice was scarcely audible. "I do, Jo-Ellen. I do still care about you." She said the words, but there was no move to go with them, no reach across to touch Jo-Ellen, to affirm that the words were true. . . .

So Deborah had her potluck suppers and her camping trips, the vacuum cleaner and the stereo. In the back of the car, Jo-Ellen carried the shorts, tank tops, blue jeans and moccasins that she was comfortable in—and a handful of more respectable items to wear job hunting when she arrived. . . . She had her sleeping bag, and the new tent she had bought, not wanting to take the expensive North Face tent from Deborah, who was the one who really loved the outdoors. The new tent was cheap. Not light enough for back-packing. No flysheet. The tag had read, "Sleeps one." She hadn't even used it yet. She'd spent the past nights in cheap motels.

Her original idea that this might be half a pleasure trip—sightseeing and camping along the way—had not been working out. She had scarcely made any stops, barreling relent-lessly through the early summer landscape without remembering anything she'd seen. In the day it was all right—driving until her arms and back and neck ached. At night, she couldn't hold up any more, couldn't pretend. Each night, she had cried herself to sleep.

Towel, washcloth, toothbrush. Soap. Letter paper and some stamps. But all she had sent was a couple of post cards. One to the gang back at the print shop, the last place she had worked. One to her mother. She had tried to write to Deborah and couldn't. Not even just to say that she was "all right."

She remembered standing on the steps outside the flat on Ashland Avenue. At her feet sat the canvas satchel that Deborah had surprised her with, full of cheese and fruit, packages of trail mix and expensive crackers. She had thanked Deborah for it and now she didn't know what she needed to say—something final, complete, to let Deborah know she meant to draw everything to a close. Finally, she attempted a decisive move—stooping to pick up the bag—at the same moment that, abruptly, Deborah reached out toward her. There was an awkward, embarrassing fumble, and a brief release of laughter. Then Deborah put her hand on Jo-Ellen's arm. Her face was full of caring, the way she used to look at Jo-Ellen a long time ago. "Are you going to be all right, Jo-Ellen?"

Jo-Ellen didn't know the answer. The moment stretched be-tween them, one last thin thread. In a sudden rush, she wanted to forget the whole thing. Unpack the car, move back in and promise, *promise* that it would be different now. Deborah's eyes were wide with anxiety. Her high forehead, between the flanks of glossy, black hair, was etched with worry lines. "I want you to write," Deborah said.

"Yeah. I will." She gave Deborah's arm a squeeze. "I'll be all right. I'll be fine."

"Just fine," she said out loud now. Her own voice sounded rusty and hollow alone in the car. The rusty hollow voice of a thirty-three-year-old woman, alone, who had broken up with her lover, quit her job, and left town. The voice of a woman who was on the way to the legendary Pacific coast, where she was going to be just fine—but who had been driving for days, crying through nights, felt like she was on speed, and probably looked a wreck. She shook her head, spread her fingers and thrust a hand back through the thick short blond hair that fell over her forehead. She could feel it flop back stubbornly a second later.

The small enclosure felt lonelier than ever, now that she had spoken, and she reached across to flick on the radio. She knew that she was somewhere past halfway across the continent, but had no idea how far she was from the nearest town. She drove with one hand on the wheel, the other guiding the tuner knob through a maze of static. A green light on the dashboard flicked on, off again, then on to stay. Oil. She couldn't remember the last time she'd added any, or whether she had a can in her trunk. She needed to pay more attention to what she was doing.

II

She pulled into a Gulf station on the outskirts of the next town. The attendant was a boy about seventeen, in a faded blue coverall and a haircut that made him look like a recruit for the U.S. army. She got out of the car, watching while he punctured the can of oil and turned the spout down into the opening in the tank.

Stretching out her cramped limbs, Jo-Ellen realized that she was not only tired of driving, but hungry. "Do you know of any good

places to eat around here?" she asked the boy. "Where I could get
a late lunch—or early dinner, I guess." She had no idea what time
it was. Only knew she had gotten on the road about eight-thirty
this morning.

He scratched his forehead with a greasy finger, then attempted
to rub out the damage with the back of his hand. "Fisher's Diner.
That's where most of the truckers stop." He pointed past the far
end of the lot. "It's about a quarter mile further, at the next junction." He turned back to Jo-Ellen, squinting in the bright sunshine,
and indicating the blue and gold plates on her car. "You from New
York City?"

It made her smile. "No. Just Buffalo. That's about as far away
from New York City as you can get and still be in the same state."
She caught the disappointment in his young face, and asked
quickly, "What about you? Did you grow up around here?"

He squared his shoulders a bit, and a grin broke across his face.
"Well, you could say that. My folks live up by Emerson. But I
come down here to work every summer. All the guys do, 'cause
the money's so good. And there ain't nothing to do in Emerson."

Now he had finished cleaning her windshield. He took the bill
she gave him, and came back a minute later with her change.
When she waved as she pulled out, he called after her, "Have a
nice trip, now."

Her eyes flushed with sudden tears. Those were the words nobody had said when she left. Deborah had wanted to know that she
would be all right. The crew at the print shop had teased about
how envious they were. Jan and Betsy had interrogated her about
reasons and plans. How could she be sure she wasn't running away
from herself?

There was nothing she could be sure of. She was not even sure
there *was* a Pacific coast. . . .

She found Fisher's without any trouble—a rather nondescript
relic of the time when diners were supposed to resemble railroad
cars, surrounded by yards of packed brown dirt. It was mid-
afternoon, and quiet inside. A couple of tired looking men, their
tattooed biceps showing under the short sleeves of their T-shirts,

sat over cups of coffee in the booth at the far end. Jo-Ellen slid onto a stool at the empty counter and a short, plump woman with salt and pepper hair came wiping her hands on her apron to hand Jo-Ellen a menu. Through a window to the kitchen, Jo-Ellen could make out a man about the same age, with more heft and less hair, but whose face matched the woman's in dogged resignation. Ma and Pa Fisher, she guessed. And now a teenage kid with mousy brown hair, neither long nor short, a checkered apron and saddle oxfords, who had to be their daughter.

She came through the swinging door from the kitchen carrying two full plates and holding the door open with the hip and shoulder of a figure that already hinted at the matronly proportions of the older woman. While Jo-Ellen surveyed the menu, she could hear the comments of the truckers as the girl served them. "Thanks, hon." And then, "Hey, sweetheart, could you bring us some ketchup?"

The same kid brought Jo-Ellen's order when it was ready— everything piping hot. The French fried potatoes were homemade—crisp and greasy just the way she liked them. And the coffee was so good she asked for a third cup.

Half an hour later, she swung the car back onto the main road that unrolled through what was left of the place—one intersection with a signal, a high school, a railroad crossing, then open country again. It wasn't much of a town.

Deborah would have called it a village, found it picturesque. Deborah would have wanted to stop and look for the public library (she worked in a library), to have a talk with the librarian, make a "connection". . . .

"You've got to make some sort of connection, Jo-Ellen," she had said, one of the evenings when they had sat on Jo-Ellen's bed in the dismal fourth floor room of the Y residence hall on North Street. "You've got to take some risks with your life—try something you've never done before. Take up karate or—become a working member at the Lexington Co-op or—" she glanced around the dreary cubicle as if searching for better ideas. There were only the cardboard boxes that Jo-Ellen had not yet bothered to unpack, the dirty laundry piled in the corner. She turned back

to Jo-Ellen, her voice urgent, palms up with fingertips out-
stretched. "You can't cower here in this . . . cell for the rest of
your life! Something has to matter to you."

"You matter to me," Jo-Ellen said.

"Oh, I know that, Jo-Ellen." Deborah's hands dropped heavily
into her lap. "You see, that's just what I mean. That just isn't
enough to get through your whole life on. I can't be that important
to you."

"You are." Jo-Ellen tried to engage her, reached out to take her
hand.

But Deborah had jumped up, and begun to pace the seven or
eight feet of linoleum tile. When she stopped again, it was at the
far end of the close space, her back against the pastel cinderblock
wall. "I can't be," she said. "I can't be everything to you. I can't
meet all your needs. I can't."

Later, or maybe it was a different evening, they had sat on the
bed together, trying again to talk things out. Deborah drew the
end of her braid forward, curling it around her finger. "Tell me,"
she said, "What did you do all the time before you met me? What
did you do at night, and on the weekends?" She waited, but Jo-
Ellen was tongue-tied. It was not only that she couldn't remember.
There was also the sickening sinking feeling that anything she said
would be turned into evidence in Deborah's hands, turned around
and somehow used against her.

Finally she said, "That was a long time ago."

"Yeah, I know." Deborah sighed, nearly smiled, and for a second Jo-Ellen almost felt that they could be together, in the old way
again, that it was just within her grasp. She tried to meet
Deborah's smile, but it had already vanished.

"But the thing is," Deborah was off on another tack now,
"that's where the trouble began. We never should have gotten so
close, in the first place, and started spending all our time together
the way we did. . . . It wasn't healthy. . . ."

"We were in love!" Jo-Ellen protested. The words left a hollow
in her chest, constricted her throat. They sounded like the end of
the chapter—a memory.

"Do you remember," she plunged on hastily, desperately, "do

you remember that night, when I still lived on Breckenridge Street, and you walked all the way over from Hertel Avenue in the snow, in the middle of the night, by yourself, because you just wanted to be with me? Remember? I had that bottle of Stone's Green Ginger Wine I'd bought because I liked the name. And I made you drink it, to get warm. God, that stuff was awful. Remember, Deb?"

When Deborah didn't answer, didn't look at her, she went on, anyway. "Remember the first time we went to Zoar Valley? The night we saw the Northern Lights? Just before you went to sleep, you said you wished every day could be like that one, for the rest of your life."

Deborah had slid off the bed beside Jo-Ellen, and stood with her back to her. She seemed to be watching the rain drip down the outside of the single grimy window. And would not answer. . . .

The sun was inching down the too blue sky, and Jo-Ellen pulled the visor to shut the glare out of her eyes. A second later, she noticed the light on the dashboard—on again. Or had it ever gone off? She watched it for a couple of moments, checked back two or three seconds later. It was steady as a pilot light. Either the car was leaking oil or something worse was wrong. Whichever, it was senseless to go on. There might not be another town, even the size of the one she had just passed, for miles. She slammed her foot into the clutch, jerking the gear shift down to pull onto the shoulder and turn the car around.

III

The boss of the kid who had sold her the oil directed her to Duncan's Auto Sales and Service, the one place in town that worked on foreign cars. Duncan was a lean, lanky character somewhere between thirty and sixty—it was impossible to tell. His gray eyes and thin, preoccupied face did not seem to register any urgency about the situation. After an unhurried but brief look, he commented conversationally that when that little green light went on, there was a dozen or more things might be wrong. But that it didn't make too much difference which one it was right now, since they closed up at five o'clock sharp. Maybe he'd get to it tomorrow, maybe not till Thursday. She could park it right over there, next to that blue pickup.

She locked the door of the car from the outside, extracted her key, and was seized with panic. She was locked out—alone in a town where she knew no one, where there was nothing for her to do, no place for her to be. The remainder of the day loomed endlessly before her. Hours until the sun set, at this time of year. Then there would be tomorrow to get through. And what if something serious was wrong, if they had to wait for parts from another city, or something worse?

Slowly, she began to walk away from the car, still gripping the keys in her hand. There were hardly any keys left on the ring now. Just the two car keys—which she would have to surrender to Duncan tomorrow—a single ancient key to her mother's apartment in Albany, and the soft circle of leather with the interlocking women's symbols that had been Deborah's first gift to her. She fingered its familiar texture—the lush, grainy suede against her thumb, the raised emblem on the smooth surface beneath her forefinger. She had given Deborah the keys to the flat on Ashland Avenue.

That had been the hardest part about saying goodbye to Deborah. Handing back the keys and making absolute what she had known for months now—had known, really, since she first moved out—that they would never get the house.

The house—it was the first thing Jo-Ellen had thought of that snowbound afternoon on the couch, when Deborah had first suggested that maybe they needed to live apart for awhile.

She remembered the impact, like a sudden blow on the head, stunning her breathless, speechless. "Let's quit pretending," Deborah had said. "You're not happy and neither am I."

Deborah seemed to have thought it all out—all of the reasons why this would be good for them, a healthful change, a growth process. "You'd get to know yourself better," she finished up confidently, "and maybe figure out more about what it is you . . .

really want to do . . . with your life.

"And that way, whenever we did get together, it would be special. . . ." She hesitated, and then added, "the way it used to be."

Jo-Ellen had sat silent throughout Deborah's explanations. They were both still on the couch under the window, but had drawn apart now, so that no part of their bodies was touching. Deborah's voice had stayed calm, rational, and Jo-Ellen felt herself shrinking smaller and smaller into the corner of the couch, not coming up with any logic to present her own vision of things. Deborah made it all sound so sensible, but Jo-Ellen felt as if she were out on the other side of the window, wandering with sinking steps in the high snow. When Deborah's voice stopped, Jo-Ellen said, "What about the house?"

"The house?"

"Yeah." She tried to sound as calm as Deborah, but a tinge of recrimination crept in. "The house in the country." With the woodlot and pasture and the creek running across their land. The grape arbor, the herb garden, the wooden swing on the porch. . . . In the magical days when they first fell in love and poured out delightful fantasies to one another on long walks in La Salle Park, they had planned every detail. But neither of them had spoken of it for ages.

Deborah was playing with the end of her braid, twisting the shiny, thick lock of hair around and around her finger. Jo-Ellen waited, hoping crazily that Deborah would say, "Maybe later, when we live together again. . . ."

"I guess I've been thinking for a while now," Deborah said, "that we should stop putting our money together. We could divide what's in the bank and each take half."

It was generous, when Deborah got paid nearly twice as much by the Buffalo and Erie County Public Library as Jo-Ellen made at the print shop. "But I didn't mean the money," Jo-Ellen said. "I just meant. . . ." she hesitated, not knowing how to say what she did not want to give the reality of words to. "How will we ever be ready to buy a house together if we can't even live in the same apartment? If we can't have this, what can we have?"

They regarded each other silently from opposite ends of the couch. Outside the window the sun shone weakly, and gusts of snow swept across the porch and drove in sudden bursts against the window. Deborah said, "We can still have a relationship. Jan and Betsy don't really live together. That house on Kenmore Avenue belongs to Jan and the kids. Betsy's always kept her apartment in Allentown. And they've been lovers for nine years."

"Nine years! And that's what you want for us? Do you think that's what Betsy and Jan really want? Do you think they're living that way out of choice? Don't you think after the kids are grown and it doesn't matter any more what the neighbors think, don't you think they'll want. . . ." she broke off, realizing she didn't really know what Jan and Betsy wanted. Maybe it was only what she had projected onto them the whole time she had known them—a future, a goal, a someday to be constantly moving toward, however slowly, a final coming together in a place to stay. What *she* wanted. A happily ever after.

She kept believing in that point in the distance where everything came together and was resolved, like the vanishing point in a picture, or the destination of the sure straight white road that had lain before her all this journey. But the road had given out and left her stranded in this absurd, vapid, empty town, which did not seem to be anywhere—only someplace along the way.

She had been walking, not paying attention to her surroundings. She was at the Gulf station again. The same boy was still on duty, and he listened sympathetically to the progress report on her car. She asked if there was a movie theater nearby.

"Not in town. There's a drive-in, about fifteen miles south of here. I guess that don't do you much good." He thought a second, and then offered, "There's gonna be a big dance over at the high school Friday night."

She went back to the diner for dinner. Now the lot was full and the place was crowded. Nearly all of the customers were men— tough looking truckers who filled the space with the clatter of utensils and loud talk. There was one empty booth, and she slid into it gratefully. After she gave her order, she found that she had to go back outside again, to get to the rest room.

She fumbled for the pull string of the light bulb, annoyed—they probably had a perfectly good bathroom indoors that the family used. The closeness of the cubicle brought every detail close. There were cobwebs in the corners, and no paper. Graffiti covered the whitewashed walls. "Maria y Carlos" inside a lopsided heart. "Andy loves Dottie." And a collection of short words that summed up her own feelings pretty accurately. She rinsed her hands quickly—at least there was water coming from the tap—and reached to open the door. Her heart leaped.

Drawn in thin black marker on the back of the door, at eye level, very small, was a double women's symbol. It stood out among the other messages as though lit up in lights—a totally unexpected welcome in this unlikely situation. Another lesbian had been here. Perhaps another woman alone, passing through on her way to the coast, like Jo-Ellen. She had stood in this exact same spot, gone out this door to eat in Fisher's Diner. She must have driven here under the same relentless sun, parked her car in the same lot, maybe walked, too, about the drab streets of this dead-end town.

As Jo-Ellen stared at the symbol, she noticed suddenly that there were words near it, written with the same black marker, "If you know what this means, talk to Kay."

She thought about them as she reclaimed her seat in the diner, as she ate the salad and chili she had ordered. "If you know what this means. . . ." It was almost like those notices she had seen so often scrawled in telephone booths. "For the best job in town, call Sally. . . ." Only, the person who had written this was a lesbian. It gave her a confused mixture of annoyance, shame, bewilderment.

". . . Talk to Kay." Who was it for? Truckers? Women truck-drivers, she supposed. But there was no phone number. . . . It was a puzzling curiosity, a crazy riddle she had no way of finding the answer to.

She spooned the chili slowly, thinking she ought to make the meal last as long as she could. There was nowhere else to go, once she left this diner.

The room was still crowded, still noisy. In addition to the racket from the kitchen, the loud talk, someone had put money into a jukebox and treated them all to a heart-broken country lament. People had to shout to be heard.

"Hey, sugar, let's see a smile on that pretty face!" Annoyed, she turned in time to see the waitress smile obediently. She didn't blame the waitress—a petite young woman who couldn't be one of the Fishers. She probably needed the tips. But it made Jo-Ellen angry all the same. Everywhere, women were decorations—when they weren't seen as prey. She pressed closer to the wall side of the booth, knowing these men would see her as easy prey, too, if they noticed her here. Even easier if they knew she had nowhere to sleep tonight in this town.

". . . Western omelet, very dry, double order of potatoes . . ." the same waitress was shouting back to the kitchen.

Now Ma Fisher was shouting to the kitchen, too. "Hey Joe! Send Kay out here with some more clean cups and plates."

A minute later, the girl in the gingham apron pushed through the swinging door, her round face flushed from the steamy kitchen and her solid arms weighted down with the wire crate full of china.

IV

For perhaps two hours, Jo-Ellen walked around the town, seeing it now for the first time. There was hardly a tree in the whole of it. Not a flower, not a blade of grass, except on the high school lawn. She had thought it didn't matter where she ended up, on this journey, but what if this town was it—the end of the line? And what if this town had been the starting place as well as the finish—all there ever was? What was it like to spend your life here waiting tables, pumping gas, washing dishes in the back of your parents' diner?

No one was on the streets. The town was suspended in the hush of the deepening evening. The houses that lined its streets were small, frame constructions, each with a picket fence that closed in a yard of dry brown dirt. Churches guarded the street corners. The drugstore, the post office, the hardware shop were all closed up for the night. There was, of course, no hotel.

On the far side of the railroad tracks, the houses were smaller, the fences weathered gray and missing slats. Then there were no fences at all. Many of these places seemed abandoned, but in front of one a lone child scraped in the dirt—a little Mexican or Indian girl who looked up at Jo-Ellen with huge, questioning eyes. Behind her, the door opened, sending a shaft of light across the yard. A taller version of the same child leaned out and called something in a language Jo-Ellen did not understand. The door opened wider, and Jo-Ellen caught a heavily spiced aroma, maybe onions and garlic frying. . . . Then both children disappeared inside.

She walked slowly, up one side of a street and down the other, studying every doorway, every shadow, every lighted window. When she passed by Fisher's Diner the windows were bright, and there were Mack trucks pulled over in the yard. She thought about the message on the wall. And the unlikely girl whose name was Kay.

Jo-Ellen slept in the Volkswagen—badly. She woke early, unrested, with a stiff neck and her body cramped with kinks. The usual headache was back, and that bottomless sense of dread that seemed to surge in, every day now, once she was fully awake. As soon as the place opened, she left the keys at Duncan's. For breakfast, she went back to Fisher's.

From the booth in the corner, she watched while the morning crowd thinned and departed. She found herself absorbed in watching the girl in the checkered apron. Kay. Jo-Ellen heard the name called again in Ma Fisher's thin, irritated voice.

"You didn't fill up none of the sugars at the tables this morning, Kay. I had to do it myself."

The kid ducked her head and mumbled some kind of answer Jo-Ellen couldn't hear, went on about her work. Her face was expressionless, impassive. Mechanically, she cleared the tables, loading the dirty dishes with their residue of crusts and peelings into a big plastic bin, swiping at the cleared tables with a limp gray rag. She didn't look as if she especially like her work, but she didn't seem to mind it, either. She seemed more or less resigned.

The words Jo-Ellen had read the night before ran through her mind. This morning, in the washroom, she had read them again: "If you know what this means, talk to Kay." It couldn't be the same Kay. This placid, obedient girl, her eyes downcast, her hands rough and chapped, with the fingernails bitten down, quietly laying flatware atop the white rectangles of napkins. It couldn't be—but it must be. What could she know about lesbians, growing up in this out-of-the-way crossroads? Why had she left that message? And what was Jo-Ellen supposed to do about it?

The cup of coffee really wouldn't last any longer. Jo-Ellen finished the last swallow, counted out coins for the tip, and paid her bill.

At the drugstore, she bought the morning paper. She read it sitting on the steps of the high school, surprised at the extent of her interest. Unemployment was still high. Demonstrators in the area were trying to get nuclear power plants closed down, just as they were back home. The local telephone service was planning to raise its rates. She read on through the ads and editorials and, finally, the classifieds. Besides pumping gas or waiting tables, a kid fresh out of high school around here could try selling vacuum cleaners, cosmetics, or encyclopedias. Most of these golden opportunities were not even in this town; the daily paper was from the county seat fifty miles away.

In the afternoon, she wandered around the streets again. They seemed drugged into stillness in the thick midday heat. There was only an infrequent passing car, only the sporadic thin wail of a child, the occasional slap of a screen door. Her wandering had brought her again to the far end of the town, where the railroad tracks divided even this scant community into two halves. The single line of track stretched in its fixed directions. East, she supposed, and west. The railroad. The only way, once, to leave this town. Maybe the only way, still, if you didn't have your own car, if you were just a kid, leaving home for the city, for the first time, trying to escape from a life that would never go anywhere. Did trains even run here any more?

She followed the railroad tracks about a mile to an old abandoned passenger station. It was dilapidated like the empty houses in town, the bleak weathered gray that the elements had left it. Behind ancient wrought-iron scrollwork, the windows were boarded up, and the doors were shuttered and nailed, too. Under the eaves, birds started and flew at her approach. She tried to imagine who would have waited for trains here. Women in pompadours and high button shoes, their belongings packed in round-topped trunks, hatboxes and carpet bags. . . .

She had carried her blue overnight bag and Deborah's backpack that one summer when she had taken the train to Albany. She remembered the unfamiliar, new feel of the pack's padded strap on her shoulder. Her hand kept moving to touch it, adjust it. It was like a secret she carried right out in the open—perfectly obvious and yet invisible. Neither her mother, nor anyone else in Albany would know that the brown backpack was really Deborah's. But Jo-Ellen would know. That summer was the first they were together.

Because everyone else was in the waiting room, they had waited on the platform in the sticky heat, the sun scorching their bare shoulders and legs. Deborah's firm limbs were brown with sun, her bare feet brown in their leather sandals. The light woven cotton of the blouse she wore clung damply to her figure. Under the thick spiral of braid that was pinned above it, the back of her neck seemed pale and vulnerable. It made Jo-Ellen think of the delicate inside surface of a sea shell. She had longed to press her lips against that smooth, fleckless stretch of skin.

They had held hands, not caring, for once, who might be watching, and could not take their eyes off each other's faces. They hardly spoke.

Once, Deborah had sighed a long sigh, and Jo-Ellen said quickly, "You don't have to wait the whole time."

Deborah had smiled and said, "I know that."

When the train pulled in, with engine roaring and a loud clamoring of bells, they had held each other tightly, as if this separation would go on much longer than the single week Jo-Ellen would spend with her mother. Deborah's eyes were bright with wetness, and Jo-Ellen brushed tears away, too. "I wish you could come with me."

Deborah said, "I know." And then, "Some things we'll still have to do alone."

They had gone on holding each other, while the other passengers hurried around them and the platform emptied, while the distorted words on the loudspeaker ran through the names of the towns across New York State. Syracuse . . . Utica . . . Schenectady . . . "I love you."

"I love you, too."

They had been so happy. She had forgotten how happy they had been.

Behind her, now, the abandoned station house stood deserted in the searing sun. The flat land stretched before her to meet the horizon. Everything was spread open, thoroughly exposed. It came to her as frank and plain as the wide open landscape: All of that was over. She was here, alone.

She remembered what Deborah had finally said that afternoon, against the conductor's shouting, and smiling across tears. "I guess I'm going to have to let you go." Jo-Ellen leaned her back against the weathered boards while tears once again filled her eyes, her throat. She shut her eyes and let the tears come.

She was back at Duncan's a quarter of an hour before they closed. He made her wait for the whole fifteen minutes while he disappeared into the garage. When he returned, it was with the same preoccupied expression on his thin face, but with a bill in his hand.

She was astounded. "It's finished?"

"Yep, all done. Thought you might have a cracked crankshaft in there, but you was lucky. All I had to do was replace the rod bearings. This figure here is for the parts, and that's for the labor. . . ."

She listened, still astonished, then dug in her pocket for the traveler's checks. He gave her back her key ring. She was free to travel on.

So now it was the road again. She drew a deep breath, fitting the key into the ignition and taking a last glance around. And then she stopped, without turning the key. She didn't have to go anywhere tonight. What she wanted to do was to have another bowl of chili for her dinner, and then just to be in a quiet place outdoors for a little while longer. And she didn't have to do anything else.

V

She walked toward the setting sun, out to the western edge of town, to the railroad station again. She walked slowly, knowing the way, now, and knowing she would find the place the same as it had been in the afternoon, as it must have been for years. The shadows of the fences, the telephone poles were long, now, and the air was faintly cooler. She reached the station and walked toward the far end of its platform, past the ancient building. And caught her breath sharply.

Under the glowing red sky, the place was completely transformed. The land was a paper fan stretched all the way open, painted with colors she had never seen before. She dropped to the edge of the platform—the concrete still warm from the afternoon sun—and stared, amazed at the deepening browns and crimsons, the last bright touches of gold: the rest of the continent.

She thought about the explorers, and the ancient notion that the world was flat, and that one could walk to the end of the earth. She had the sensation of having arrived at that edge—to find not a void, not a chasm, but another world, newly opened, lying waiting. While she watched, the sky turned from red to violet to deep ink blue, and filled with a silent storm of stars.

When she finally went back to the car, it was to get her sleeping bag. Not the tent. She would sleep on the desert under the stars.

VI

She woke in the morning to find herself and her sleeping bag drenched with heavy dew, her face and arms itchy with swollen insect bites. But she felt a strange sense of elation, adventure. She was wide awake and her head was clear. She would get some breakfast and in another hour be back on the road, a hundred miles away before half the day was up. She dumped the wet sleeping bag over the back seat of the Volkswagen and drove back to the diner. Turning into its nearly empty lot, she realized she must have slept late.

Inside, she hardly noticed Ma Fisher behind the counter. Instead she watched Kay clear the tables, the stolid, deliberateness of her motions, the quiet patience in her face. Someday someone—some woman—would spark that patience into expectancy, anticipation. That plain face would be transformed with excitement and pleasure.

The last couple of men paid their bills at the counter and left. Ma Fisher's solid figure trundled into the kitchen, the door swinging shut behind her. The girl poured a fresh cup of coffee and filled a small pitcher with cream. She brought them to Jo-Ellen's table.

The place had grown quiet with that heavy daytime silence that settled over this town like the thick dust settled in the yards of its houses. Jo-Ellen finished her eggs and hash browns and asked for another coffee. From the back room, she heard a radio come on— a man's voice holding forth, followed by organ tones and the blended strains of a choir. It must be ten or eleven o'clock. She had no reason, any longer, to be in this town. She couldn't linger forever—should get moving. While she swallowed the last of her coffee, she pulled the keys from her pocket, playing with them in one hand. She let them fall, clinking softly, one by one, against each other, thumbed the worn circle of suede while her forefinger traced the raised insignia on the other side.

She didn't know what it was about Kay. She knew it was not attraction. It was something else—some sense she had gotten that, as well as endings, there were places where people began. That this town, barren and lifeless as it had seemed, was one of them. There was nothing, really, to connect her and this girl—just a bit of graffiti on a washroom door that might have been written by or read by anyone. But she felt the connection—and because of it, some small sprout of hopefulness about the rest of her life.

Kay was back with her check pad. "Anything else?" she asked without looking up, already adding the figures. There was still no one in the room except the two of them. Jo-Ellen watched Kay's hands—the stubby fingers gripping the ball point pen, pressing hard to go through the carbon—until the girl looked up, impatient.

"No," Jo-Ellen said. "That's all." The girl slapped the check face down on the table and moved away. Jo-Ellen lingered just a minute longer in the booth. Then she slid out onto her feet.

She backtracked to the Gulf station one more time and asked for a map of the state. Opening the map out on the hood of the car, she stood for a few minutes studying it. If she stayed on this route, there was a city that seemed pretty sizeable that she might be able to make by nightfall. Or she could turn south at the next major junction, and take a smaller highway that went through a state park. . . .

Behind the wheel again, she fitted the key into the ignition. The few remaining keys felt sparse in her hand. They were all that was left on the key ring now—three keys. The soft piece of leather with its interlocking symbols was gone. She had left it after breakfast, face up on the scarred black surface of the table, along with her change.

She traced a finger across the long blue line, then folded the map and placed it on the seat beside her. She shifted into gear. A moment later she was pulling back onto the highway.

The Saints and Sinners Run

My name is Cecily Banks and I drive on the South Street line: Number 40, from Parkside to Society Hill. I work full time—five days a week, and been driving long enough to be off any Saturday or Sunday I want. But the fact is, I rather work on Sunday than any other day. Sunday I don't be worrying about my kids.

Any week day, soon as it get close to three o'clock, I'm starting in to think about them. Wonder if Tammy remembered to wait for Marvin. Hope she didn't lose her key again. Like the last time, when it was pouring down rain, and she was too embarrassed to tell anybody and made Marvin sit on the back step with her so wouldn't no neighbors see they was locked out. I'd been home calling neighbors for half an hour before I figured out where they was.

Wonder if she got any homework—and if she does, I hope she starting to do it, and not gonna wait till I get home, then claim she forgot. I hope they had enough to eat for lunch, and don't eat up the leftovers in there I got planned for tonight's dinner.

Some nights I'd like to call home, just tell Tammy to stick something in the oven. Can't you just see a whole bus fulla people waiting, while I get out at the corner pay phone: "Honey, set the dial at three hundred. And open up the icebox door. Now, you see that piece of ham on the second shelf, wrapped up in tin foil? That's right. And down at the bottom there's a bag of string beans. . . ."

It's only a couple of hours from when they get out to when I get off. But those the worst two hours of my day. Schoolkids! Kids today take the prize for being the most impudent, insolent, sassy, brassy, rowdy, rambunctious, and downright fresh of any generation there ever was. We thought we was bad, when we used to get smart with people or answer back. But that little bit of rebellion wasn't nothing, compared to what you see today. And hear.

Friday, a girl wasn't no bigger than my Tammy tried to get on at the front door with a big old cone in her hand, piled way up high with soft custard. I say, "Miss—" I always start out treating them respectful, for all the good it does— "Miss, you can't bring that on the bus." I point to the sign up front, where it very clearly say "No Eating. No Drinking." Of course, I know half these kids can't read, even if they is in junior high, but she can hear me talking to her. She just flash her pass at me and try to march on by. Only the bus is so crowded it ain't exactly easy to slide past, and don't nobody move over to let her by.

"Miss, did you hear me? I said there's no food allowed on this bus."

And she explode. "I ain't deaf. I heard you. But I just spent a M-F-ing dollar on this ice cream cone. How'd I know the M-F-ing bus was gonna come. Don't never come on time no other day. And I got a right to get on this M-F-ing bus. I got a M-F-ing pass."

I say, "Miss, you entitled to your opinion about the bus company regulations. But I just get paid for doing my job. You're gonna have to get off and wait for the next bus."

Lucky for me, she stomps on off the bus. Sometimes it ain't so easy. Sometimes they be slipping them passes from hand to hand so fast you'd think they was doing magic tricks. I've had women's pocketbooks and men's gold chains snatched. I've had to stop everything from break dancing contests to knife fights. Half the time, I'm shaking in my shoes, but I always act real tough. I'll take em on if I have to. I grew up in South Philly myself.

Just this past Friday, way early in the morning, I was pulling off over the South Street bridge when I caught a whiff of smoke. Don't nothing else in the world smell like that—I know it's got to be weed. I can see in my mirror where it must be coming from—a collection of gym bags and long legs in sneakers with the tongues hanging out, sticking way out in the aisle. I turn around. One of em, look like he the ringleader, leaning way back in his seat behind a pair of shades, like this TWA and he cruising at an altitude of 25,000 feet: Mr. Kool himself.

Now I ain't necessarily saying I object to the stuff—in the right place at the right time, with the right company. But the Southeastern Pennsylvania Transportation Authority ain't the right company. "No smoking allowed on the bus." I say it once and it don't make no impression. I say it again, little louder. "There's no smoking allowed on this bus. If you want to smoke, you'll have to get off the bus and do it somewhere else."

We ain't even talking about *what* they smoking. Like I say, I always start out treating em with respect. But some kids don't even know what respect is. So finally I pull on over by the University Stadium, flick on the flashers, and get up and stride all the way to the back of the bus. It gets real quiet. Every kid on the bus got their eyes glued on me, watching to see what I'm fixing to do. Cept of course Mr. Kool & Company—when I get back there they all casually looking out the window, just like they was actually passing some scenery.

Somebody musta put the joint out—ain't nobody even exhaling back here. But I give my rap anyway. "No smoking on the bus. No pipes, cigars, cigarettes, cigarillos, or unidentified illegal substances. Now if you fellas want to smoke you get off the bus. If you want to stay on the bus, you follow the rules." I look around at all of em, but nobody say nothing. So I start back up to the driver's seat. And sure enough, soon as my back is turned, somebody got something to say.

"What's wrong with joint?" some kid sing out. "God made it." And a shot of laughter goes hooting all through the bus.

Now most of the time I just hold my temper and keep my mouth shut, cause I know how hard it is to get the best of these kids. But that time I forgot myself, and I hollered out, just like I was back on my old block down in South Philly, "That's right. God made it. But he didn't plant none on my bus."

The kids all make that noise they make when somebody score one, and I step on the gas and roar off before anybody got time to figure out what the next move gonna be.

Now you can see why I choose to work on Sundays whenever I can. No smartass kids trying to mess with my head. And my own two smartass kids safe at my mama's, and she don't let em mess with *her* head. Sunday mornings on the bus, everything is calm, peaceful, and orderly, just the way I like it. I call it The Saints and Sinners Run—nobody out but the ladies, on the way to church. They flick out their senior citizens' cards and parade on past in their printed silks, white gloves, and little veiled hats, treating me to my own private fashion show.

I pick em up all along Parkside and on through West Philadelphia, and then all the way down South Street, one or two on every corner. Seem like, no matter where people move to, they always want to come back home to their own church, the one they was raised up in. It always gets me thinking about the church I was raised up in myself.

Sunday mornings in the springtime, right around this time of year, the church ladies looked just like a garden. Our little church'd be overflowing with all the pretty colors, just the way those same ladies' little fenced-in back yards'd be overflowing with roses and peonies and snowball bushes all summer long. I used to sit there all starched and ironed, and straightened and curled, and listen to the pipe organ starting up with those long, slow notes, and watch the light come slanting in through the colored windows—and I knew why they called that room the sanctuary. There wasn't no question in my mind that that was where God spent his Sunday mornings. God and all the angels, too.

So I like to do that South Street run, because it takes me back. What I like to do is call out the names of the different churches, along with the streets I call out all the other days. Everybody enjoys that. It makes em feel real special, feel recognized—and also kinda lets em know that I respect what they doing, that my working on Sunday don't necessarily mean I don't abide by the Ten Commandments. Somebody got to ferry people back and forth, so they can worship where they choose on the day they choose. And I see that as my mission.

Once in a while, an old lady will ask me, "Don't you go to church?" She'll be looking up and down my slacks and my man-tailored blueshirt. But that's my uniform. She can see it's pressed clean and fresh on Sunday, just like every other day. And I may have a no-nonsense hairdo, but it's neat and trim.

"Yes, ma'am," I say. "When I don't have to work." It's not exactly a lie. The times I go to church *do* be times when I don't have to work. Maybe not *every* time I don't have to work, but she didn't ask that.

"What church you belong to?"

And I say, "North Star Baptist Church." I joined North Star when I was ten years old. I ain't unjoined yet, so I guess I'm still counted among the congregation. And that's always the end of that. She nod her head and smile at me, and go find her a seat on my chariot.

"Twenty-third Street. Gray's Ferry Avenue. Saint Anthony DePadua Chapel." That's an early morning stop, for folks that want to get their church going out of the way. "Church of the Lord Jesus Christ of the Apostle Faith. Apostolic Square." The Apostolic church is a different story. Some of the folks I drop off there'll stay all day. The kids that attend that church is something else—the boys talking in quiet voices, young girls slender, dark and pretty, in their hats and long skirts. They mind their mamas, and their little brothers and sisters mind them. I wish more of their kind would ride on my bus during the week. We still in Saints territory.

"Twenty-second Street. New Central Baptist Church. Twentieth Street. Saint Philip's." Sometimes I think South Philly got the highest concentration of churches in the whole country. Only thing they got more of is bars. I guess when the churchgoing folks saw how fast new bars kept opening up, they figured they just had to go on opening up new churches, to try to keep the balance even. "Nineteenth Street. Holy Trinity Baptist. Saint Mary's Episcopal." Every other week I call Saint Mary's first, so the Episcopalians won't think I'm playing favorites. Though I don't suppose they ever lose any sleep worrying over the Baptists, anyway.

"Seventeenth Street. First Colored Wesley Methodist Church, one block to the right. New Light Beulah Baptist Church. Truevine Church of God in Christ." We getting into sinners territory now. It always tickles me how some folks like to go to church feeling holy, and others would rather see themselves as sinners. It must be easier on the sinners—they don't have to put so much into keeping up the image all week long. And the sinners always sound like they having a better time during services, too, making all those joyful noises unto the Lord. Truevine is just a little church, not much more than a storefront, but they got a powerful sound you can hear all the way from South Street.

"Fifteenth Street. Wesley AME Zion one block to your left, on Lombard Street." And I holler out the names like that, all the way on down through Society Hill. Finally I wind up down past Mother Bethel. Then swing back around to Lombard Street. And that's my run.

This morning start out like any other Sunday. Only thing is, I don't seem to pick up nobody along the way but old ladies. Not even no middle-aged ones. Come to think of it, it *was* pretty cloudy this morning when I started out. Only the most faithful servants gonna turn out today, the kind you can identify as church-folks a block away, even on a weekday.

When I get to Market Street, there's a whole flock of plump, healthy looking sisters in white matron's uniforms, waiting for me. And then the next stop, here comes a woman remind me of my grandma—thin as a twig, in a prim gray dress with little white flowers scattered all over it, and a gold cross around her neck. Hardly five feet tall, with a little blue hat perched up atop her head, and a great big huge straw pocketbook. Next corner, I pick up two or three more. Cloudy days don't bother me none, and I'm feeling pretty good this morning, right on schedule and singing to myself. "Good news, chariot's a coming. . . . "

While I'm waiting for the light to change, I smell something that distinctly smell like fried chicken. And I can hear somebody crumpling those crispy papers all around, getting it out. I take a deep whiff. Mmm-hmm. Hot fried chicken and french fries. I can even smell a little barbecue sauce. I been kinda daydreaming, not paying attention or remembering what day it is. And the next thing I know I'm on my feet, heading for the back of the bus, with my speech already forming in my mind.

Sure enough, somebody got a paper bag opened up, and a paper napkin all spread out in their lap, and their mouth open just getting ready to chomp into a big old piece of fried chicken. Only thing wrong is who it is—that little gray wisp of a woman remind me of my grandma. She looking up at me with that piece of chicken between her fingers, and her feet not even touching the floor. She may be little and skinny and old, but she got a look in her eye make you stop and think twice about what you got to say to her.

"Ma'am," I start out.

"Yes?"

"Uh, ma'am. Excuse me ma'am." I can't seem to get no more words out. Cause the way I was raised up, you don't mess with nobody could be your grandma.

"Yes? What is it?" Kind of voice used to put the fear of God in me.

"Uh, um . . ." And then I take a chance and look all around the bus for a second—no, there ain't nobody here cept churchgoers. No kids that ride the bus on weekdays, might remember this. "Well, excuse me, but was you the one wanted to get off at Thirteenth Street?"

She look me right in the eye, like she know I just made that up, and say, "No, I was not."

And I'm backing back to the driver's seat, mumbling "Scuse me, ma'am. Sorry to trouble you. Just want to make sure nobody don't miss their stop." I step on the gas and holler out, "Twelfth Street. Saint Peter Claver."

I guess the good sister'll finish her fried chicken in her own good time. And I guess she know what stop she want, and she'll manage to get off when she get there. Obviously she don't need no help from me. And I say to myself, "Just drive the bus, Cecily, that's all you gotta do; that's all you getting paid for—just driving the bus. Ain't nobody gonna know what go on on this bus but you and these saints and sinners here, and God. Just stop for the red light. Go when it turn green. Put your wipers on now, it's starting to rain a little bit."

And right that minute I smell it. That thick burnt odor come snaking through the air, all through the bus right up to my driver's seat. It ain't frankincense. Only one thing in the world smell like that—and I don't never allow nobody to smoke it on my bus. Ain't nobody ever tried to before—on Sunday morning!

I got my foot on the brake again, pull back on the hand brake and turn around in my seat. And all there is is gray-haired ladies, wearing crosses and carrying Bibles, with their legs crossed at the ankle and their hands folded in their laps, and the sweetest, most innocent expressions on their faces you ever did see. I look em all over, and every one of em look me back right in the eye. And I shake my head—and turn back around in the driver's seat. Muttering to myself. "Just drive the bus, girl. That's all you getting paid to do."

I don't know which one it was. I don't want to know. Cause even just thinking about somebody's grandma smoking joint on the bus does a job on my head. There's certain things you come to depend on about the way the world supposed to operate. When I see some teenage kid with a twenty pound radio on his shoulder, I know he ain't gonna be reading no Bible on the bus. But this morning the hoodlums and the saved souls all mixed up together in my head. Used to be I could tell em apart. Now I don't know what to expect. I can still smell that distinct aroma, hanging in the air, all the way down to Mother Bethel.

When I get to the end of the run, I park the bus and shut off the motor to take my break. And then go cross the street to a telephone booth, and do something I ain't hardly ever done, all the years I been working for the Transportation Authority. I dial my mama's number.

"Hi, Ma. Cecily here."

"What happened, honey? What's wrong? You have an accident? You all right?"

I'm feeling kinda silly already, and not exactly sure why I did call. "No, nothing's wrong. I just got to thinking about the kids . . . and you, wondering if . . . everything's O.K."

"Now you know better than that." I can hear her voice get all huffy, the way it does when she's insulted. "You know you don't need to worry about Tammy and Marvin when they're with me. You oughtta save your quarters for something you might need em for."

"Yeah, I guess you right. I just thought I'd see how you all was getting along today. Uh . . . how's Grandma doing?" My grandma just moved in with my mother a couple months ago.

"She's fine. I'm fine. The kids fine. Everybody doing just fine. You better go get yourself something to eat, before your break is up."

"Yeah, I am." Don't seem like much left for me to say. "Uh, would you put Tammy on the line a second?"

Seem like she get real quiet all of a sudden.

"Tammy's not here right now."

"Not there?" What I feel like is like somebody come up and laid a nice friendly hand on my back—and then clobbered me over the head. "Not there?"

"Now just calm down. She's not here because she went to church. Her and Marvin both went."

"They went to church?" It don't sound too likely. Church ain't never been Tammy's favorite place to be on a Sunday morning. Marvin's neither.

"They didn't go by themselves. They went with Grandma. Out to Fifty-ninth Street."

"Fifty-ninth Street?" Nothing is making any sense.

"Yes. You know. To her old church. Fifty-ninth Street Baptist Church. And Cecily, it ain't gonna harm those two none to get a little Christian training now and then. It ain't gonna hurt em at all."

I can't think what to say. I oughtta feel reassured. But I'm still feeling clobbered. Like things ain't in my own hands any more.

"Look," she says. "You know Tammy and Marvin just as safe with us as when they with you. You know Grandma wouldn't let nothing happen to her babies. So just set your mind at rest."

After I hang up the phone, I wander back cross the street and climb on up in the driver's seat. She's right. Shouldn't be nothing wrong with a nice old lady taking her two great-grandkids to church on Sunday morning. I turn on the lights, start up the motor, open the doors. But my mind is not at rest. I keep thinking about Tammy, Marvin, Grandma . . . the schoolkids and the church ladies, like they all part of a puzzle I can't figure out—don't know where to start. Wonder what *do* go on in all these churches. I always thought I knew.

When I zip past Thirty-eighth Street, somebody's grandma is tapping me on the shoulder, saying, "Excuse me, Miss, but isn't this bus supposed to turn on Thirty-eighth?"

And it's a good thing she did it, too. I'd a been clear out to the Fifty-ninth Street Baptist Church by now.

In the Deep Heart's Core

I

Those places up the coast had wonderful names. Point Reyes.
Mendocino. Inverness. That last one always made Sahara think
of the place in the Yeats poem, The Lake Isle of Innisfree:

I will arise and go now, and go to Innisfree.

Sahara came to this part of the country for the first time when she
first struck out on her own. Twenty years have passed since then,
and now she has returned. She has come back to a particular place,
this time. But that first time, twenty years ago, she traveled up and
down this road for no better reason than that she liked the sound
of the names.

At the end of one of those long ago days, she had stood by a
roadside, hitchhiking. She'd had no luck the past half hour, and
had walked maybe two or three miles already along the road, turning to stretch her arm out straight every time a car passed. There
was gritty sand in her socks. Sand had worked its way under her
kerchief and settled in her scalp, among the thick, coarse crinkles
of her hair. Sand clung beneath her nails and lined the pockets of
the faded smock she wore over her patched up blue jeans. She
stood with her feet planted far apart, and was glad of her big-
boned frame, taking up its space, glad of her height—her size letting them know she could take care of herself. Being outdoors all
summer long had bronzed her face from tan to copper brown, and
she was glad of it, the earth color distinct to everyone who passed,
glad of who she was.

Night was coming. The sun slanted red, sinking over the ocean side of the road. Watching it, she had seen the foot path that led off down the bank. She had crossed the road and followed it. She didn't know that there was another way in, a steep rutted drive a little ways up the highway. She had been surprised to find the space the path led her to scattered with colorful cars and vans.

Where she found herself was not on the beach she had expected, but on an enormous wide plateau, a grassy place that was open and expansive, yet sheltered and hidden. It was walled on one side by the sandy banks that led up to the road. She had walked through the long grass, across to the other edge of the open field, and found that the land ended abruptly in a sudden drop down a sheer cliff to the sounding ocean hundreds of yards below. She stood at the edge; the wind whipped through her, and she could see far out to sea. Later, someone told her it was as far west as you could go. The Headlands, she found out they called it.

It was a place where people gathered—folk traveling up and down the coast. Some of them were on holiday—summer gypsies who'd return to some snug town place in a week or a month. Others, in ancient khaki garb and run-down boots, looked as though they had been on the road all their lives. And there were a few who, like Sahara, seemed to be just finding a place from which to begin. They had come in beat-up cars or housecars—pickup trucks with handmade houses perched on their beds—in battered, rusted-out vans and panel trucks, or brightly painted ones. Some, like her, had come walking or hitchhiking, everything they still cared about owning on their backs. They would stay a night, a week, make friends, make love, make decisions about their lives, move on.

Now, twenty years later, Sahara is one of those who has driven here—in a battered blue van. She is not sure why she is back on the road. Or for how long. She did not give notice at the school where she has worked for the past five years. But when she closed up her classroom in June, packing the supplies away, scrubbing the chairs and cots, taking down the posters and bulletin boards, she felt that it was the last time. She couldn't keep on, year after year, loving a whole new class of children, then letting them go.

When she set out in her van at the start of this summer, it seemed there was something drawing her back to this place she had found quite by accident so long ago. It seemed there was something calling her here, some voice that did not stop. Was it the ocean, sounding night and day against the cliffs down below the Headlands, the ocean calling to her? She doesn't know—only knows that if she stays, time will tell why she has come back.

She has been here for three nights and three days now, and has found that twenty years have not changed the place much. Traveling people have not forgotten it. At night someone will build a fire and people will share whatever they have. It is nearly night now. Sahara has taken the largest pot, and gone across the road for water.

Down the road, she first sees the girl, standing where a car has just left her off. The girl faces the traffic that doesn't come, her boots planted far apart. The sun is in her eyes, but she doesn't shade them, and she doesn't take the pack off her back and let it down to rest in the sand by the side of the road. She hasn't a sign with a destination on it. But she does have a map—draws it out of her back pocket and opens it out. She turns to look back up the road and then moves her finger across the map. She folds it to a different square, studies it a little longer, and shoves it into the back pocket of the brown corduroys.

A moment later, she notices the path sloping down the bank between the scrubby bushes, just across the road. Sahara watches the way she hitches up the pack a bit, then looks up and down the road. And Sahara knows the girl is imagining a soft beach to sleep on tonight, high above the level of the tide, just as Sahara did when she first came to this place, very young, on foot, and alone.

Sahara would have been called a girl then, too. Now there is ash gray in the short hair that is tied up beneath her fringed kerchief. Under the spigot, the water splashes over a network of tiny wrinkles on her hands. And when she lifts the pot, the veins stand out on the back of her hand and arm. Her skirt sweeps the grasses as she follows, in long, even strides, down the path where the girl disappeared.

Already, there is a ring of faces around the firelight. Whatever they have brought, they will share. Some nights there is little. Wild peas someone has gathered along the road, thrown into the stew. Abalone or a little fish. Wild berries. Other nights, people stopping have brought food, and there is plenty.

This is one of the nights of plenty. There's meat, and someone has brought fresh sourdough bread.

Two long-haired children tag each other in and out of the firelight, until the smell from the big pot finally draws them in and settles them still.

The girl from the roadside has found her way to the gathering and is standing at the back of the circle. Someone calls out to her, "Come on over by the fire. Pull up a chair."

The girl shows a brief flicker of a smile, and moves in next to Sahara. The sudden closeness of her changes something in the air, draws Sahara to an alertness, an awareness that feels like wakefulness of a part of her that has been asleep. She feels, too, as if she's wise to something the girl doesn't yet know — having watched her on the road, maybe. She feels there is a reason the girl has chosen her, out of the circle, to sit beside — some reason the girl herself is not conscious of. She turns to speak. The girl's eyes are wary.

"I'm Sahara," Sahara says. And then, "If you've got a cup or a bowl or something, you might want to get it out."

A big woman in overalls with a blue star tattooed on her arm is ladling out the stew. She holds up a wooden bowl and someone says, "Over here," and the bowl is passed that way. When she gets to the girl's blue and white enameled cup, someone says, "It's his," jerking a thumb over beside Sahara.

The girl shakes the hair out of her eyes and reaches to take the cup. "Hers," she says with half a smile on her lips. But she says it so softly that only Sahara hears it.

To Sahara, it's clear that the girl is a womanchild, nearly a woman. It would have been, even in this gathering darkness, even if Sahara had not seen her on the road. Perhaps her clothes are deceiving. Besides the boots and corduroys, she is wearing a denim jacket with the sleeves cut off. There is nothing on her arms, and there seems to be nothing beneath the jacket. She hasn't any breasts.

But her face is a woman's face. The brown eyes are wide and uncertain, and her mouth, even just smiling halfway, changes the whole look into something so far from harshness you know she is somebody's daughter. Beneath the locks of short brown hair, Sahara can see tiny drops of silver in her earlobes. The girl's skin is tanned. Her face makes Sahara think of a locket—a heart-shaped locket shut tight on a secret.

She knows she has never seen this person before, and yet she can feel herself straining to place her, to figure out who she is. She watches the girl, and the girl watches silently while the others talk.

"I'm thinking about going up around the Russian River, see if there's any work in the lumber business."

"I don't know. Up in Oregon, where I come from, people been laid off that worked there thirty years."

A baby wakes and starts to cry. A woman reaches to take it from its father, holds it in the crook of her arm and lifts up her sweater on one side.

Sahara looks away. It hurts her to watch that—something she will never have now.

"Brought the whole family this time, huh?" Someone says to the father with a grin.

"Oh, yeah. Even brought the kitchen sink. We live in that yellow pickup over there. That little fella's never lived in a house, and I hope he never will."

Sahara watches the girl next to her as her eyes follow the man's finger, over to the cabin that is perched on the back of the pickup, with its gabled roof and stained glass windows and domed skylight. The girl's eyes widen, and she keeps on looking at it for a long time.

The talk eddies and swirls around them. The fire burns lower. Some people depart for the cafe in the town, a few miles away. And the children are put to bed. The girl's backpack would make a fine backrest or pillow, but she sits bolt upright, with her back straight. Her legs are crossed, and every part of her is stiffly still.

Only her fingers never stop moving, itching, twisting around one another, clasping and unclasping, opening and closing. She stares into the fire. The firelight flickers and leaps in her womanchild's face, in her wide eyes.

Sahara knows she must be the one to begin. In her low voice, she phrases one of the two age-old questions of the road. "Where you from?"

The girl startles from the trance of the fire, and turns to look at her. In the moment that it takes, Sahara imagines herself as this girl must see her. Old. To someone as young as her, Sahara's near forty years will seem much older than they seem to Sahara. The girl won't see the gray that salts her hair. It's covered with the bright gold kerchief, tied like an Arab headdress, hanging down her neck and back. But even in the firelight, she'll see the lines in Sahara's face, the crow's-feet at the corners of her eyes, and likely the hairs on her chin. She will see old. And black. An old black woman in dowdy clothes from a second-hand store, with a gaudy headrag wrapped around her head. She won't see who Sahara really is.

The girl has turned back to stare at the fire, after answering the question with just one word. "Oakland."

Sahara watches her a minute more. It is the girl's fingers that won't be still in her lap, that finally make her go on and ask the other question.

"Where you headed?"

She sighs a long sigh, and says, "Just traveling." But she draws up one knee to lean against and turns to Sahara.

"Me, too," Sahara says, smiling. "Just traveling, this time. You been on the road long?"

The girl shakes her head from side to side. "I just left home. This morning."

"No kidding? This morning? For the first time?"

"Yeah. Well, I ran away a couple of times before. But I was just a kid. This is different. This time I won't go back there. Ever!"

"What happened?" As soon as she's said it, she knows it's wrong. And the girl, who'd turned to face her, now jerks her gaze away, back to the fire.

"It was just time for me to leave, that's all. It wasn't really my home anyway. It was my grandparents' place. And it was time for me to get out, that's all." Now she has drawn up the other knee, her arms wrapped tight around, so that her shape is a hard, stiff triangle.

"I guess that time comes for everybody," Sahara says. "Everybody who's ever going to be her own person." She stares into the fire, remembering how it was. "I left home when I was eighteen. My mother thought the world of me, and tried to give me everything, but it wasn't enough for me. I had to have something of my own." She had always meant to go back and set things right with her mother, years later when she would be an equal, married, with children of her own, when the things they had quarreled over wouldn't matter any more. She'd always thought there'd be plenty of time for that and then, one summer, when Sahara was halfway around the world, her mother had suddenly died. . . .

"I went on the road, too," she tells the girl beside her. "That was all I wanted to do. Hitchhike cross-country. Get out to California. Didn't know the first thing about how to do it. I mean, I didn't even know how to read a road map right to get out of my home town. First time a tractor trailer ever stopped for me, I didn't know how to climb up there. I didn't know some pretty basic safety stuff I ought to've known either. Like to check the locks on the doors of the car before you get in, make sure you can get out." She's eyeing the girl's profile, hoping she's listening, wishing she'd ask what else. There's so much Sahara knows now that would have made things easier, if someone had told her. "Or even," she says, "to always go to a woman if you get in trouble and need some kind of help. Don't ever depend on a man." She waits, but the girl doesn't answer, doesn't ask. And Sahara knows how scared she is.

People are returning from the town. Somewhere, someone picks up a guitar, and a quiet song spills out of the nearby darkness. Sahara stands; her skirt falls in billows to the ground. She stretches, reaching her hands out for one last feel of the fire's warmth, then moves away, to do the things she needs to do for the night.

She collects her sleeping bag from the battered blue van and comes back by way of the fire, crouching for a second beside the girl. "You got a sleeping bag? Or blankets or anything?"

"Huh? Oh, yeah. A sleeping bag."

"It's a good night for sleeping out," Sahara says. "I've got an old van here, but I only use it when it rains." She nods her head over toward the far side of this grassy place, away from the road. "I always like to sleep out there, on the Headlands. In the morning when you wake up, you can look right out over the ocean."

"I think I'll just stay here awhile longer," the girl says.

"Got a lot on your mind to think about, huh?"

"Yeah," she says. "Yeah, I guess so."

"Well, if it helps your thinking any to talk, come over and talk to me. I'll be awake a bit longer. And I wake up easy, too. I don't mind—if something's troubling you." She smiles at the girl, trying to let her know that she wants to be a friend.

"Thanks," the girl says. And smiles back—a self-conscious smile, but a whole one, this time. It makes Sahara feel as if a door has suddenly swung wide open in this night, a door into a bright, new place that has never been entered.

The wind is high, blowing shreds and shards of gray clouds across a three-quarter moon. Sahara places her sleeping bag with the head facing the bluffs. She turns her shoes upside down and makes a pillow, under the sleeping bag, of the sweater she has taken off. Then she lies still in her bag, on her back, and lets the memories come flooding in. It is the children that she is always remembering, all the children who have passed through her life.

II

The first time Sahara went to sleep in a house where she was alone with children, she had a hard time sleeping. In her head she went over in detail the whole layout of the house, with its abundance of doors and halls and private baths. She did not know it as well as she should, and wondered if she could really find her way if there were a fire and she was half asleep.

The Weatherbys had not bothered to question how she might deal with emergencies, or even ask what her experience had been. They had looked at her and not seen a teenager who had never done anything like this before. They had seen, in her dark face and her tall, womanly frame, only generations of cooks and "help," nursemaids and nannies. . . . The interview with Mrs. Weatherby hadn't even taken fifteen minutes. The woman was so overjoyed at finding someone on such short notice, so relived that she would not have to cancel the week in the Bahamas after all, that she had explained all this in much greater detail than she explained about Heather's temper tantrums or Bradley's asthma.

In the stuffy little spare room, Sahara worried until she couldn't keep her eyes open any longer. Three hours later she was wide awake, as though a voice had called her. Down the long hall, there was only silence, but she threw on her robe and padded in her bare feet to the rooms where the children slept.

Peter Weatherby was hunched in the middle of his bed with the covers pulled over his head. He was crying. Sahara sat by his side and rubbed his back in wide, slow circles. She did not want to talk or sing, afraid she might wake the others. So, very softly, she recited poems to him—"The Owl and the Pussycat," "Wynken, Blynken and Nod," "Little Brown Baby"—all the ones that her own mother had read to her, over and over again. Her hand kept stroking the warm dampness of his soft pajamas, circling in the rhythm of the verses—until he slept.

Still she sat there, a long time after, watching the mound of his small body rise and fall in gentle regularity. He had cried. And she, at the other end of the hall, the other end of the house, had not heard, but had known. He had cried and she had put him back to sleep. It was as if she had passed through some ritual, some initiation. . . .

*

In the night, there are only quiet noises, the ocean at the foot of the cliffs, and the dry grasses rustling. The wind is restless still, whirrs in Sahara's ears and washes her bare face cold and clean. Overhead, most of the clouds have blown off and stars are out.

The ancient rhyme comes into her head. "Starlight, starbright, first star I see tonight. . . . " She has always made the same wish, over and over, on every star and wishbone, every milkweed seed caught and dandelion blown away, on all the birthday candles. Whenever she head the words "heart's desire," she thought of a child.

She never wanted a man. And she chose a way of life—without men—in which children did not easily appear. Sometimes it seems she has spent her whole life finding ways to get close to other people's children.

*

The child who did not know how to play was a little girl, a Puertorriqueña. Her name was Elizabeth Maldonado. She was three. Elizabeth's mother came into Sahara's classroom holding her small daughter's hand and gazed around the colorful playroom. She spoke to Sahara in a voice barely loud enough to hear. "*Mi hija, mi Elizabeth*—*no sabe jugar*. She is not like my other children. She does not play. *Es la única cosa*—that is the one thing I care about . . . maybe . . . you can teach her?"

In the playroom the children clustered around the sandbox that stood on tall legs by the window. They patted up mountains and highways, scooped out tunnels and lakes. Their high-pitched voices bargained and traded, cried for a turn with the dump truck, shrieked with delight.

Elizabeth stood in the center of the room, a crumpled tissue in one hand, a tiny doll house figure in the other. Her slender body swaying in the short cotton dress, she rocked rhythmically heels to toes, toes to heels. There was a whisper of a smile on her face; her eyes were far away.

When Sahara got closer, she could hear her humming—a tone-less tune that never began or ended, just went on and on. Sahara stooped to the little girl's level and lightly put an arm around her shoulders, smiling into her eyes. "What's that you have in your hand, Elizabeth? *¿Qué tienes en la mano? Ah —una muñeca.* Can you say that? *Muñeca. ¿Es tuyo?*"

On the playground those first weeks of fall, the other children would come tumbling over to her, short brown and tan and pale legs pumping, untied sneakers and soft plastic sandals pounding across the asphalt. "Teacher!" "¡*Maestra*!" "Miss Sahara!" "Elizabeth doesn't want a turn to ride." "Can I have Elizabeth's turn, Miss Sahara? Please?"

"Oh, no. Elizabeth *needs* her turn. Where is she? *Vente, Elizabeth. Ven acá.*" Taking her by the hand, she led her to the tricycle, while the little girl lagged back and shook her head. "Come on go for a ride. We'll go slow—*muy suave.*"

Come, Elizabeth. I'll climb the sliding board with you. I'll touch the sticky paste first. We'll pat the rabbit together. . . .

In January, Franklin crossed the playroom, his chestnut round face more pleased than angry. "Hey, you know what, Miss Sahara? Elizabeth talked to me. She said, 'You go away!'"

Another day, Manuela came crying. "Elizabeth took the baby's bottle. I had it first." In the playhouse corner, Sahara could see Elizabeth, tangly brown hair curtaining her face, slight figure bent over the carriage, holding the plastic nursing bottle to the baby doll's mouth.

There was an afternoon on the playground again, nearly the last week of school, and the end of the day. Across the street she could see Mrs. Hughes waiting for the light to change, and Franklin had seen her too, was already collecting his paintings and the wooden airplane he had made. Down the block, Mrs. Maldonado came pushing the baby's stroller in front of her.

Sahara looked around for Elizabeth. The little girl was just starting up the ladder of the sliding board. She was always very serious about this, hands clamping the railings, patent leather pumps stepping one rung at a time, her small chin set with determination. Sahara stopped her for a second with her hand on the child's back. "When you get up to the top, look and see who's coming."

The child reached the summit. She stood between the high arched railings, a hand on each one, and scanned the horizon. And her tiny face broke into a furious grin. "¡Mami! ¡Mami! ¡Mira, Mami!"

She swept down the shining length of the slide, landing on her feet and ran, brown hair flying, ran laughing across the entire playground, out the open gate, and into her mother's arms.

*

Sahara will never forget the image of that little girl, arms open, laughing and running—away from her. She will not forget any of them, though years have passed, and they are scattered in different cities all across the country. Quiet nights in open places, the boundaries are unguarded, and they come back to her. Peter and Elizabeth and so many others. Like Joy.

*

Sahara lived with Joy, Joy's mother Janet, four other women and two other children in a big sprawling old house in the heart of the city, maybe ten years ago, now. Joy was another child who couldn't play. Tamika and Nicholas would be racing up and down the stairs after school, calling out to each other and shouting. "I can't find my skate key!" "Hey, will you hold the door while I get my bike out?" "Wait up! Wait for me!"

Joy's delicate dark fingers closed only with straining effort around a crayon or pencil, and the pictures came out a snarl of faintly marked scribbles. Bikes and skates, even scissors and puzzles were impossible.

Tamika and Nicholas ran in and out—for a piece of chalk, a glass of water—the door screen banging behind them. Sahara sat on the couch with Joy in her lap, the soft pile of Joy's short hair against her cheek, and read picture book after picture book. "And when he came to the place where the wild things are they roared their terrible roars. . . . "

"And gna-a-ashed their ter-ri-ble tee-e-eeth . . . ," Joy's small voice drawled, forcing out the syllables one by one with effort. The words came out distorted, but she had them all memorized. After

living with her for a month, Sahara could understand almost everything Joy said. It was like listening to words slowed down on a tape
recorder that she could speed up in her head. Or like learning to
decipher someone's handwriting. "And ro-o-olled their ter-ri-ble
eye-s. . . . "

"And showed their terrible claws." Outside, she could hear
Tamika and her girlfriends.

"That ain't the way you draw a hopscotch, girl. Onesies posed
to be all by itself." "I'm first, when she get finished." "Nu-uh! I already said it."

Tamika and Nicholas were only a year and two years older than
Joy. But they didn't play with her. Sahara had heard one of
Tamika's friends asking once, just outside the window, "How
come your sister still has to be in a stroller?" And Tamika declaring
hotly, "That's not my sister!"

Nicholas and Tamika had quickly made friends with each other
and made their own friends in the neighborhood. Their friends
lived with mothers and fathers, or mothers and brothers and
sisters, or even with grandmothers, but not with multi-ethnic col-
lections of odd assorted women who weren't related to them or to
each other. Their friends were never invited in, by either Tamika
or Nicholas.

" . . . And into the night of his very own room where he found
his supper waiting for him and it was still hot." She closed *Where
the Wild Things Are* and slapped it down on the pile on the floor
below them, spilled Joy onto the couch and stood up. "That's it.
I'm not reading any more stories. Know what we're gonna do
now?"

"Wha-a-at?"

We're gonna sail away. To where the wild things are."

A table turned upside down was their boat, the broom and mop
were oars. Joy steadied the sail and kept a sharp look out for islands on the horizon. Sahara rowed and sang "Heave Away
Santyanna" and "The Sloop John B." They caught fish with one of
Joy's long shoelaces. And then Joy dropped the sail, her palms pat-
ting the upturned underside of the table beneath her. Her eyes

were pools of dismay. "O-oh no-o."

"What is it? What's the matter?" Sahara was instantly alert, the play forgotten.

"It's we-et."

Sahara began to pat the floor too, feeling anxiously around Joy's bottom. Everything was absolutely dry. Joy heaved out a guffaw of laughter at Sahara's antics and finished triumphantly, "I think we sss-pru-ung a lee-e-eak."

They were busy bailing out when Nicholas came in, and didn't notice him until he walked through the ocean and right up to the side of the boat and said, "Hey what are you doing? How come you turned over the table?"

"This isn't a table," Sahara corrected.

Joy grinned and said, "If you do-on't sstart sss-wim-ming you're go-ing to dro-o-own."

""Can I play?" Nicholas asked.

Sahara nearly answered, but Joy cut her off. "I kno-o-ow." Her voice was loud and sure. "He can be one of the wi-i-ild things."

*

Whatever became of them? Joy would be fifteen or sixteen now, Nicholas maybe eighteen. But the house had broken up at the end of the first year. Eventually, she had lost touch with all of them.

When Sahara sleeps, she dreams of children. Babies and children—they come to her in dreams every night. Each is distinct and different from any other. Each has her own voice, his own shape, her own face like no one else in the world.

III

Something has awakened her on this night, just as it did on that first night long ago, knowing that one of the children was awake, and in trouble.

She listens. The wind has died as it always does, along toward morning. The night is absolutely still. Only the tops of the grasses rustle softly. Above her, the clouds have all blown off; the vast blackness is alight with stars, the milky way cutting a wide swath across the center. The girl has brought her sleeping bag and stretched it out on the ground along next to Sahara's.

Sahara sits up and studies the figure beside her. There's a scent of dye and fresh fabric from the sleeping bag—it must have been bought new for this adventure. Its inhabitant lies still, with her face turned away and half covered. Sahara knows she is crying.

She hesitates, torn over whether to allow the girl her space, or to enter it. Where does she belong in this person's life? Does she belong at all? Finally she reaches out and rests a hand for a moment on the girl's shoulder through the thick, quilted material. "I'm awake," she says, "if you want to talk about it."

The girl doesn't answer at first. Then her voice comes out, scratchy with tears. "That won't help."

"Maybe not. Maybe it won't change anything. But if you tell someone, then at least you don't have to carry it all by yourself." She waits a moment, then goes on. "You know, that's one of the things I found out is so special about the road—it keeps your secrets for you. You can talk to somebody you just met and tell them anything. After tonight you never have to see me again." She waits a bit longer, then asks, "What happened?"

"Nothing," the girl says.

"I mean back at home—*something* happened."

"I just had to get out of there, that's all. It wasn't my home, anyway. They never let me forget *that*."

"Did they . . . did your grandparents throw you out?"

The girl has squirmed to sit up, wiping her face with the heels of her hands. Now she laughs a laugh that is like a handful of stones thrown down on concrete. "I told him not to bother. The bastard. I told him not to waste his breath. Said I was capable of walking out that door without any help from him. And I did it, too."

"Something he did made you furious. . . . "

"Everything he did drove me crazy! He's always so smug and proud of himself—he can't ever let me forget it for a minute how they took me in and raised me. I'm supposed to be humble and grateful for the rest of my life." She let another pebble of hard laughter fall. "That's not giving."

"Every time I do anything he doesn't like, any little thing, he goes crazy. He said I was going to end up just like her." She turns, suddenly, to seek out Sahara's face in the darkness. "My mother, I mean. I'm gonna end up another disgrace to the family. Ashamed to come home." Her eyes hold Sahara's in the quiet, charcoal darkness. "He calls her a slut. Right to my face. He says that about my mother! He says I'm gonna end up a slut just like her."

She looks away again, out into the night. Her hands have begun to play with the edge of the quilted fabric, pleating it into harried ruffles, letting it go, taking it up again. "I didn't even do anything. He won't ever give me a chance to explain. Him and his dirty mind. Just because I was out all night he thinks I was screwing around. I wasn't even with a boy. I was with Marianne Delarosa. Just cause I like to talk to her. We were up talking all night, sitting in her brother's truck."

She is silent for a few moments, looking out over the distance, out over the Headlands where, far below, the voice of the ocean is suddenly loud, sounding against the rocky wall of the cliff. For a moment, everything about the girl is still; even her fingers lie resting.

"Everybody says my mother ran off with another woman. Some woman she met over in the city that nobody knew. But they won't ever tell me any more than that. They act like it's something I'm not supposed to know. My grandparents won't talk about it at all. Except to point out how I'm turning out just like her." Her fingers close on a clump of grass beside her and rip the long blades from the ground, tearing them into bits. "So what if I *am* like her? I'm *supposed* to be like her. She was my mother! She got out of there when she was eighteen and I swore to God I would, too."

"That must have hurt you a lot," Sahara says softly. The locket face turns to her; the girl looks surprised that Sahara is still there. "The way she left you there, I mean," Sahara says. "That she got out herself, but she didn't take you—she left you there."

The girl is brushing sudden fresh tears back from the sides of her face with the heels of her hands. "It doesn't matter," she says.

"Because I got out now, too. And I'm going to find her."

"Your mother?"

"Yeah. That's really why I left—and where I'm going."

"So she stayed in touch with you?"

"Well, not exactly. We haven't been in touch. But I know she was supposed to have gone up north. Headed for Vancouver. That's what everybody said."

Sahara looks over to check her face, but the girl is completely serious. She's leaning on one elbow now, her look full of that confidence in herself that doesn't last long past eighteen. "Vancouver's a big place," Sahara says softly.

The girl seems not to have heard. "And I know what she looks like. Everybody says I look just like her."

"Of course," Sahara says gently, "she'd be older now."

"Of course," the girl answers, lightly.

"And she must have lived through a lot. I mean, she may not be the person you think she is. . . . "

"Then I want to know who she is, now. I want her to know who *I* am."

And Sahara thinks, no, *you* want to know who you are. You want her to give you that. And she never will, even if you find her. No one can.

"Whoever she is," the girl says, "I don't care. She's my mother. I'm going to find her. I don't care if it takes me the rest of my life."

Now the girl is lying back, with her arms folded under her head, watching the sky. "Sure are a lot of stars out here," she says, and her voice sounds hushed and small against the vast night.

Sahara slips down in her bag and turns on her back to view them, too. "Sure are. It's funny to think how, down here, they all look close together and pretty much the same. But up there every one is different, and they're millions of miles apart." She wants to go on: You might as well go wandering off into the sky, little girl, and try to find just one star.

"You know, your mother could be anywhere," she says, finally. "She could be camping out right here on this roadside tonight."

"I never thought of that. I guess she could." The girl turns that one over in her mind, and says, doubtfully, "Maybe I should stay here for awhile." Then she asks, "Are *you* going to be staying here long?"

"I don't know. I could stay a while longer." She's thinking, thinking about what happens next, in her life. She listens to the sound of the waves, striking on the rock below, striking and splashing, roaring and repeating. Something like that never-ending sound has called her back here, after all these years, to this place to begin from, begin again.

Twenty years ago, that first time, she sat looking out over these same cliffs another bright, starry night, and a woman sat beside her who seemed old to Sahara then. She was the one who told Sahara what this place was. She said, "Where we're sitting now is as far west as you can go. This cape is the end of the land, and these Headlands are the end of the cape. Everybody always wants to travel west, but when you get here you have to change directions."

Sahara lifts up a little to look over at the girl who lies watching the stars. "I might be going north in another few days," she tells her. "It's been a long time since I've been in Vancouver."

There's some kind of softness, a warmth, that has come stealing up in the windless dark and circled the two of them all the way around. Sahara feels it—something that glows and makes her happy. She wants to say to the girl: I know who you are. I knew all along—you were *somebody's* daughter. . . . Instead, she asks, "Do you like Yeats?"

The girl laughs a self-conscious laugh. "I don't know what they are."

And Sahara smiles back in the dark. "Close your eyes and listen. It'll help you go to sleep."

She chants the words softly out into the night between them, one poem and then another, until the child beside her has fallen a-sleep. She goes on to finish, anyway,

> *"I will arise and go now, for always night and day*
> *I hear lake water lapping with low sounds by the shore;*
> *Where I stand on the roadway, or on the pavements grey,*
> *I hear it in the deep heart's core."*

In The Life

Grace come to me in my sleep last night. I feel somebody presence, in the room with me, then I catch the scent of Posner's Bergamot Pressing Oil, and that cocoa butter grease she use on her skin. I know she standing at the bedside, right over me, and then she call my name.

"Pearl."

My Christian name Pearl Irene Jenkins, but don't nobody ever call me that no more. I been Jinx to the world for longer than I care to specify. Since my mother passed away, Grace the only one ever use my given name.

"Pearl," she say again. "I'm just gone down to the garden awhile. I be back."

I'm so deep asleep I have to fight my way awake, and when I do be fully woke, Grace is gone. I ease my tired bones up and drag em down the stairs, cross the kitchen in the dark, and out the back screen door onto the porch. I guess I'm half expecting Gracie to be there waiting for me, but there ain't another soul stirring tonight. Not a sound but singing crickets, and nothing staring back at me but that old weather-beaten fence I ought to painted this summer, and still ain't made time for. I lower myself down into the porch swing, where Gracie and I have sat so many still summer nights and watched the moon rising up over Old Mister Thompson's field.

I never had time to paint that fence back then, neither. But it didn't matter none, cause Gracie had it all covered up with her flowers. She used to sit right here on this swing at night, when a little breeze be blowing, and say she could tell all the different flowers apart, just by they smell. The wind pick up a scent, and

Gracie say, "Smell that jasmine, Pearl?" Then a breeze come up from another direction, and she turn her head like somebody calling her and say, "Now that's my honeysuckle, now."

It used to tickle me, cause she knowed I couldn't tell all them flowers of hers apart when I was looking square at em in broad daylight. So how I'm gonna do it by smell in the middle of the night? I just laugh and rock the swing a little, and watch her enjoying herself in the soft moonlight.

I could never get enough of watching her. I always did think that Grace Simmons was the prettiest woman north of the Mason-Dixon line. Now I've lived enough years to know it's true. There's been other women in my life besides Grace, and I guess I loved them all, one way or another, but she was something special—Gracie was something else again.

She was a dark brownskin woman—the color of fresh gingerbread hot out the oven. In fact, I used to call her that—my gingerbread girl. She had plenty enough of that pretty brownskin flesh to fill your arms up with something substantial when you hugging her, and to make a nice background for them dimples in her cheeks and other places I won't go into detail about.

Gracie could be one elegant good looker when she set her mind to it. I'll never forget the picture she made, that time the New Year's Eve party was down at the Star Harbor Ballroom. That was the first year we was in The Club, and we was going to every event they had. Dressed to kill. Gracie had on that white silk dress that set off her complexion so perfect, with her hair done up in all them little curls. A single strand of pearls that could have fooled anybody. Long gloves. And a little fur stole. We was serious about our partying back then! I didn't look too bad myself, with that black velvet jacket I used to have, and the pleats in my slacks pressed so sharp you could cut yourself on em. I weighed quite a bit less than I do now, too. Right when you come in the door of the ballroom, they have a great big floor to ceiling gold frame mirror, and if I remember rightly, we didn't get past that for quite some time.

Everybody want to dance with Gracie that night. And that's fine with me. Along about the middle of the evening, the band is playing a real hot number, and here come Louie and Max over to me, all long-face serious, wanting to know how I can let my woman be out there shaking her behind with any stranger that wander in the door. Now they know good and well ain't no strangers here. The Cinnamon & Spice Club is a private club, and all events is by invitation only.

Of course, there's some thinks friends is more dangerous than strangers. But I never could be the jealous, overprotective type. And the fact is, I just love to watch the woman. I don't care if she out there shaking it with the Virgin Mary, long as she having a good time. And that's just what I told Max and Lou. I could lean up against that bar and watch her for hours.

You wouldn't know, to look at her, she done it all herself. Made all her own dresses and hats, and even took apart a old ratty fur coat that used to belong to my great aunt Malinda to make that cute little stole. She always did her own hair—every week or two. She used to do mine, too. Always be teasing me about let her make me some curls this time. I'd get right aggravated. Cause you can't have a proper argument with somebody when they standing over your head with a hot comb in they hand. You kinda at they mercy. I'm sitting fuming and cursing under them towels and stuff, with the sweat dripping all in my eyes in the steamy kitchen—and she just laughing. "Girl," I'm telling her, "you know won't no curls fit under my uniform cap. Less you want me to stay home this week and you gonna go work my job and your job too."

Both of us had to work, always, and we still ain't had much. Everybody always think Jinx and Grace doing all right, but we was scrimping and saving all along. Making stuff over and making do. Half of what we had to eat grew right here in this garden. Still and all, I guess we *was* doing all right. We had each other.

Now I finally got the damn house paid off, and she ain't even here to appreciate it with me. And Gracie's poor bedraggled garden is just struggling along on its last legs—kinda like me. I ain't the kind to complain about my lot, but truth to tell, I can't be down crawling around on my hands and knees no more—this body I got put up such a fuss and holler. Can't enjoy the garden at night proper nowadays, nohow. Since Mister Thompson's land was took over by the city and they built them housing projects where the field used to be, you can't even see the moon from here, till it get up past the fourteenth floor. Don't no moonlight come in my yard no more. And I guess I might as well pick my old self up and go on back to bed.

Sometimes I still ain't used to the fact that Grace is passed on. Not even after these thirteen years without her. She the only woman I ever lived with—and I lived with her more than half my life. This house her house, too, and she oughta be here in it with me.

*

I rise up by six o'clock most every day, same as I done all them years I worked driving for the C.T.C. If the weather ain't too bad, I take me a walk—and if I ain't careful, I'm liable to end up down at the Twelfth Street Depot, waiting to see what trolley they gonna give me this morning. There ain't a soul working in that office still remember me. And they don't even run a trolley on the Broadway line no more. They been running a bus for the past five years.

I forgets a lot of things these days. Last week, I had just took in the clean laundry off the line, and I'm up in the spare room fixing to iron my shirts, when I hear somebody pass through that squeaky side gate and go on around to the back yard. I ain't paid it no mind at all, cause that's the way Gracie most often do when she come home. Go see about her garden fore she even come in the house. I always be teasing her she care more about them collards and string beans than she do about me. I hear her moving around out there while I'm sprinkling the last shirt and plugging in the iron—hear leaves rustling, and a crate scraping along the walk.

While I'm waiting for the iron to heat up, I take a look out the window, and come to see it ain't Gracie at all, but two a them sassy little scoundrels from over the projects—one of em standing on a apple crate and holding up the other one, who is picking my ripe peaches off my tree, just as brazen as you please. Don't even blink a eyelash when I holler out the window. I have to go running down all them stairs and out on the back porch, waving the cord I done jerked out the iron—when Doctor Matthews has told me a hundred times I ain't supposed to be running or getting excited about nothing, with my pressure like it is. And I ain't even supposed to be *walking* up and down no stairs.

When they seen the ironing cord in my hand, them two little sneaks had a reaction all right. The one on the bottom drop the other one right on his padded quarters and lit out for the gate, hollering, "Look out, Timmy! Here come Old Lady Jenkins!"

When I think about it now, it was right funny, but at the time I was so mad it musta took me a whole half hour to cool off. I sat there on that apple crate just boiling.

Eventually, I begun to see how it wasn't even them two kids I was so mad at. I was mad at time. For playing tricks on me the way it done. So I don't even remember that Grace Simmons has been dead now for the past thirteen years. And mad at time just for passing—so fast. If I had my life to live over, I wouldn't trade in none of them years for nothing. I'd just slow em down.

The church sisters around here is always trying to get me to be thinking about dying, myself. They must figure, when you my age, that's the only excitement you got left to look forward to. Gladys Hawkins stopped out front this morning, while I was mending a patch in the top screen of the front door. She was grinning from ear to ear like she just spent the night with Jesus himself.

"Morning, Sister Jenkins. Right pretty day the good Lord seen fit to send us, ain't it?"

I ain't never known how to answer nobody who manages to bring the good Lord into every conversation. If I nod and say yes, she'll think I finally got religion. But if I disagree, she'll think I'm crazy, cause it truly is one pretty August morning. Fortunately, it don't matter to her whether I agree or not, cause she gone right on talking according to her own agenda anyway.

"You know, this Sunday is Women's Day over at Blessed Endurance. Reverend Solomon Moody is gonna be visiting, speaking on 'A Woman's Place In The Church.' Why don't you come and join us for worship? You'd be most welcome."

I'm tempted to tell her exactly what come to my mind—that I ain't never heard of no woman name Solomon. However, I'm polite enough to hold my tongue, which is more than I can say for Gladys.

She ain't waiting for no answer from me, just going right on. "I don't spose you need me to point it out to you, Sister Jenkins, but you know you ain't as young as you used to be." As if both of our ages wasn't common knowledge to each other, seeing as we been knowing one another since we was girls. "You reaching that time of life when you might wanna be giving a little more attention to the spiritual side of things than you been doing. . . . "

She referring, politely as she capable of, to the fact that I ain't been seen inside a church for thirty-five years.

" . . . And you know what the good Lord say. 'Watch therefore, for ye know neither the day nor the hour . . . ' But, 'He that believeth on the Son hath everlasting life . . . '"

It ain't no use to argue with her kind. The Lord is on they side in every little disagreement, and he don't never give up. So when she finally wind down and ask me again will she see me in church this Sunday, I just say I'll think about it.

Funny thing, I been thinking about it all day. But not the kinda thoughts she want me to think, I'm sure. Last time I went to church was on a Easter Sunday. We decided to go on accounta Gracie's old meddling cousin, who was always nagging us about how we unnatural and sinful and a disgrace to her family. Seem like she seen it as her one mission in life to get us two sinners inside a church. I guess she figure, once she get us in there, God gonna take over the job. So Grace and me finally conspires that the way to get her off our backs is to give her what she think she want.

Course, I ain't had on a skirt since before the war, and I ain't aiming to change my lifelong habits just to please Cousin Hattie. But I did take a lotta pains over my appearance that day. I'd had my best tailor-made suit pressed fresh, and slept in my stocking cap the night before so I'd have every hair in place. Even had one a Gracie's flowers stuck in my buttonhole. And a brand new narrow-brim dove gray Stetson hat. Gracie take one look at me when I'm ready and shake her head. "The good sisters is gonna have a hard time concentrating on the preacher today!"

We arrive at her cousin's church nice and early, but of course it's a big crowd inside already on accounta it being Easter Sunday. The organ music is wailing away, and the congregation is dazzling—decked out in nothing but the finest and doused with enough perfume to outsmell even the flowers up on the altar.

But as soon as we get in the door, this kinda sedate commotion break out—all them good Christian folks whispering and nudging each other and trying to turn around and get a good look. Well, Grace and me, we used to that. We just find us a nice seat in one of the empty pews near the back. But this busy buzzing keep up, even after we seated and more blended in with the crowd. And finally it come out that the point of contention ain't even the bottom half of my suit, but my new dove gray Stetson.

This old gentleman with a grizzled head, wearing glasses about a inch thick is turning around and leaning way over the back of the seat, whispering to Grace in a voice plenty loud enough for me to hear, "You better tell your beau to remove that hat, entering in Jesus' Holy Chapel."

Soon as I get my hat off, some old lady behind me is grumbling. "I declare, some of these children haven't got no respect at all. Oughta know you sposed to keep your head covered, setting in the house of the Lord."

Seem like the congregation just can't make up its mind whether I'm supposed to wear my hat or I ain't.

I couldn't hardly keep a straight face all through the service. Every time I catch Gracie eye, or one or the other of us catch a sight of my hat, we off again. I couldn't wait to get outa that place. But it was worth it. Gracie and me was entertaining the gang with that story for weeks to come. And we ain't had no more problems with Cousin Hattie.

Far as life everlasting is concerned, I imagine I'll cross that bridge when I reach it. I don't see no reason to rush into things. Sure, I know Old Man Death is gonna be coming after me one of these days, same as he come for my mother and dad, and Gracie and, just last year, my old buddy Louie. But I ain't about to start nothing that might make him feel welcome. It might be different for Gladys Hawkins and the rest of them church sisters, but I got a whole lot left to live for. Including a mind fulla good time memories. When you in the life, one thing your days don't never be, and that's dull. Your nights neither. All these years I been in the life, I loved it. And you know Jinx ain't about to go off with no Old *Man* without no struggle, nohow.

To tell the truth, though, sometime I do get a funny feeling bout Old Death. Sometime I feel like he here already—been here. Waiting on me and watching me and biding his time. Paying attention when I have to stop on the landing of the stairs to catch my breath. Paying attention if I don't wake up till half past seven some morning, and my back is hurting me so bad it take me another half hour to pull myself together and get out the bed.

The same night after I been talking to Gladys in the morning, it take me a long time to fall asleep. I'm lying up in bed waiting for the aching in my back and my joints to ease off some, and I can swear I hear somebody else in the house. Seem like I hear em downstairs, maybe opening and shutting the icebox door, or switching off a light. Just when I finally manage to doze off, I hear somebody footsteps right here in the bedroom with me. Somebody tippy-toeing real quiet, creaking the floor boards between the bed and the dresser . . . over to the closet . . . back to the dresser again.

I'm almost scared to open my eyes. But it's only Gracie—in her old raggedy bathrobe and a silk handkerchief wrapped up around all them little braids in her head—putting her finger up to her lips to try and shush me so I won't wake up.

I can't help chuckling. "Hey Gingerbread Girl. Where you think you going in your house coat and bandana and it ain't even light out yet. Come on get back in this bed."

"You go on to sleep," she say. "I'm just going out back a spell."

It ain't no use me trying to make my voice sound angry, cause she so contrary when it come to that little piece of ground down there I can't help laughing. "What you think you gonna complish down there in the middle of the night? It ain't even no moon to watch tonight. The sky been filling up with clouds all evening, and the weather forecast say rain tomorrow."

"Just don't pay me no mind and go on back to sleep. It ain't the middle of the night. It's almost daybreak." She grinning like she up to something, and sure enough, she say, "This the best time to pick off them black and yellow beetles been making mildew outa my cucumber vines. So I'm just fixing to turn the tables around a little bit. You gonna read in the papers tomorrow morning bout how the entire black and yellow beetle population of number Twenty-seven Bank Street been wiped off the face of the earth—while you was up here sleeping."

Both of us is laughing like we partners in a crime, and then she off down the hall, calling out, "I be back before you even know I'm gone."

But the full light of day is coming in the window, and she ain't back yet.

I'm over to the window with a mind to holler down to Grace to get her behind back in this house, when the sight of them housing projects hits me right in the face: stacks of dirt-colored bricks and little caged-in porches, heaped up into the sky blocking out what poor skimpy light this cloudy morning brung.

It's a awful funny feeling start to come over me. I mean to get my housecoat, and go down there anyway, just see what's what. But in the closet I can see it ain't but my own clothes hanging on the pole. All the shoes on the floor is mine. And I know I better go ahead and get washed, cause it's a whole lot I want to get done fore it rain, and that storm is coming in for sure. Better pick the rest of them ripe peaches and tomatoes. Maybe put in some peas for fall picking, if my knees'll allow me to get that close to the ground.

*

The rain finally catch up around noon time and slow me down a bit. I never could stand to be cooped up in no house in the rain. Always make me itchy. That's one reason I used to like driving a trolley for the C.T.C. Cause you get to be out every day, no matter what kinda weather coming down—get to see people and watch the world go by. And it ain't as if you exactly out in the weather, neither. You get to watch it all from behind that big picture window.

Not that I woulda minded being out in it. I used to want to get me a job with the post office, delivering mail. Black folks could make good money with the post office, even way back then. But they wouldn't out you on no mail route. Always stick em off in a back room someplace, where nobody can't see em and get upset cause some little colored girl making as much money as the white boy working next to her. So I stuck with the C.T.C. all them years, and got my pension to prove it.

The rain still coming down steady along about three o'clock, when Max call me up say do I want to come over to her and Yvonne's for dinner. Say they fried more chicken that they can eat, and anyway Yvonne all involved in some new project she want to talk to me about. And I'm glad for the chance to get out the house. Max and Yvonne got the place all picked up for company. I can smell that fried chicken soon as I get in the door.

Yvonne don't never miss a opportunity to dress up a bit. She got the front of her hair braided up, with beads hanging all in her eyes, and a kinda loose robe-like thing, in colors look like the fruit salad at a Independence Day picnic. Max her same old self in her slacks and loafers. She ain't changed in all the years I known her—cept we both got more wrinkles and gray hairs. Yvonne a whole lot younger than us two, but she hanging in there. Her and Max been together going on three years now.

Right away, Yvonne start to explain about this project she doing with her women's club. When I first heard about this club she in, I was kinda interested. But I come to find out it ain't no social club, like the Cinnamon & Spice Club used to be. It's more like a organization. Yvonne call it a collective. They never has no outings or parties or picnics or nothing—just meetings. And projects.

The project they working on right now, they all got tape recorders. And they going around tape-recording people story. Talking to people who been in the life for years and years, and asking em

what it was like, back in the old days. I been in the life since before
Yvonne born. But the second she stick that microphone in my face,
I can't think of a blessed thing to say.

"Come on, Jinx, you always telling us all them funny old time
stories."

Them little wheels is rolling round and round, and all that
smooth, shiny brown tape is slipping off one reel and sliding onto
the other, and I can't think of not one thing I remember.

"Tell how the Cinnamon & Spice Club got started," she say.

"I already told you about that before."

"Well tell how it ended, then. You never told me that."

"Ain't nothing to tell. Skip and Peaches broke up." Yvonne
waiting, and the reels is rolling, but for the life of me I can't think
of another word to say about it. And Max is sitting there grinning,
like I'm the only one over thirty in the room and she don't remember a thing.

Yvonne finally give up and turn the thing off, and we go on and
stuff ourselves on the chicken they fried and the greens I brung
over from the garden. By the time we start in on the sweet potato
pie, I have finally got to remembering. Telling Yvonne about when
Skip and Peaches had they last big falling out, and they was both
determine they was gonna stay in The Club—and couldn't be in
the same room with one another for fifteen minutes. Both of em
keep waiting on the other one to drop out, and both of em keep
showing up, every time the gang get together. And none of the rest
of us couldn't be in the same room with the two a them for even as
long as they could stand each other. We'd be sneaking around,
trying to hold a meeting without them finding out. But Peaches
was the president and Skip was the treasurer, so you might say our
hands was tied. Wouldn't neither one of em resign. They was both
convince The Club couldn't go on without em, and by the time
they was finished carrying on, they had done made sure it
wouldn't.

Max is chiming in correcting all the details, every other breath
come outa my mouth. And then when we all get up to go sit in the
parlor again, it come out that Yvonne has sneaked that tape re-

cording machine in here under that African poncho she got on, and has got down every word I said.

When time come to say good night, I'm thankful, for once, that Yvonne insist on driving me home—though it ain't even a whole mile. The rain ain't let up all evening, and is coming down in bucketfuls while we in the car. I'm half soaked just running from the car to the front door.

Yvonne is drove off down the street, and I'm halfway through the front door, when it hit me all of a sudden that the door ain't been locked. Now my mind may be getting a little threadbare in spots, but it ain't wore out yet. I know it's easy for me to slip back into doing things the way I done em twenty or thirty years ago, but I could swear I distinctly remember locking this door and hooking the key ring back on my belt loop, just fore Yvonne drove up in front. And now here's the door been open all this time.

Not a sign a nobody been here. Everything in its place, just like I left it. The slipcovers on the couch is smooth and neat. The candy dishes and ash trays and photographs is sitting just where they belong, on the end tables. Not even so much as a throw rug been moved a inch. I can feel my heart start to thumping like a blowout tire.

Must be, whoever come in here ain't left yet.

The idea of somebody got a nerve like that make me more mad than scared, and I know I'm gonna find out who it is broke in my house, even if it don't turn out to be nobody but them little peach-thieving rascals from round the block. Which I wouldn't be surprised if it ain't. I'm scooting from room to room, snatching open closet doors and whipping back curtains—tiptoeing down the hall and then flicking on the lights real sudden.

When I been in every room, I go back through everywhere I been, real slow, looking in all the drawers, and under the old glass doorstop in the hall, and in the back of the recipe box in the kitchen—and other places where I keep things. But it ain't nothing missing. No money—nothing.

In the end, ain't nothing left for me to do but go to bed. But I'm still feeling real uneasy. I know somebody or something done got in here while I was gone. And ain't left yet. I lay wake in the bed a long time, cause I ain't too particular about falling asleep tonight. Anyway, all this rain just make my joints swell up worse, and the pains in my knees just don't let up.

The next thing I know Gracie waking me up. She lying next to me and kissing me all over my face. I wake up laughing, and she say, "I never could see no use in shaking somebody I rather be kissing." I can feel the laughing running all through her body and mine, holding her up against my chest in the dark—knowing there must be a reason why she woke me up in the middle of the night, and pretty sure I can guess what it is. She kissing under my chin now, and starting to undo my buttons.

It seem like so long since we done this. My whole body is all a shimmer with this sweet, sweet craving. My blood is racing, singing, and her fingers is sliding inside my nightshirt. "Take it easy," I say in her ear. Cause I want this to take us a long, long time.

Outside, the sky is still wide open—the storm is throbbing and beating down on the roof over our heads, and pressing its wet self up against the window. I catch ahold of her fingers and bring em to my lips. Then I roll us both over so I can see her face. She smiling up at me through the dark, and her eyes is wide and shiny. And I run my fingers down along her breast, underneath her own nightgown. . . .

*

I wake up in the bed alone. It's still night. Like a flash I'm across the room, knowing I'm going after her, this time. The carpet treads is nubby and rough, flying past underneath my bare feet, and the kitchen linoleum cold and smooth. The back door standing wide open, and I push through the screen.

The storm is moved on. That fresh air feel good on my skin through the cotton nightshirt. Smell good, too, rising up outa the wet earth, and I can see the water sparkling on the leaves of the collards and kale, twinkling in the vines on the bean poles. The moon is riding high up over Thompson's field, spilling moonlight all over the yard, and setting all them blossoms on the fence to shining pure white.

There ain't a leaf twitching and there ain't a sound. I ain't moving either. I'm just gonna stay right here on this back porch. And hold still. And listen close. Cause I know Gracie somewhere in this garden. And she waiting for me.